Jesse H. Butler

Home - Femme Heroic

and Miscellaneous poems

Jesse H. Butler

Home - Femme Heroic
and Miscellaneous poems

ISBN/EAN: 9783337194307

Printed in Europe, USA, Canada, Australia, Japan

Cover: Foto ©Andreas Hilbeck / pixelio.de

More available books at **www.hansebooks.com**

HOME:

FEMME HEROIC AND MISCELLANEOUS

POEMS.

BY

JESSEE H. BUTLER,

SAN FRANCISCO, CALIFORNIA.

———

BOSTON:

COLBY AND RICH,

9 MONTGOMERY PLACE.

1875.

STEREOTYPED AT THE
BOSTON STEREOTYPE FOUNDRY,
19 Spring Lane.

H O M E :

femme Heroic and Miscellaneous Poems.

DEDICATED TO

MY BRIGHT PARTICULAR STAR.

"None knew thee but to love thee;
None named thee but to praise."

FITZ-GREENE HALLECK.

CONTENTS.

PREFACE.

THE intelligent reader will discover no attempt at a Classical or an Heroic composition, or to imitate the higher flights of poetic rage, but only an expression of the common mind, in unison with Nature, animate and inanimate, and of the universal Soul in its natural life, through all the common feelings and appreciations of the good, the true, and the beautiful.

To the author, imitation would be dishonest and disgraceful ; flattery would be despisable ; oracular wisdom would be ridiculous ; and high-flown words and phrases the evidence of a low taste. He, therefore, like the lark, builds his nest on the dear old

7

Earth, as on the bosom of his mother ; and like the same unassuming little bird, flutters upward, towards the sun, singing and trembling in his own ecstasy, till exhausted, he falls back to his own quiet, lowly, humble home, to listen to the loftier songs of the thrush, the mocking-bird, or the scream of the imperial eagle ! and then twitters to his own heart, and to his dear companions — " Are we not brothers all ? "

J. H. BUTLER.

HOME.

INTRODUCTION.

YE heavenly powers, that float around
Where beauty dwells, and love is found;
That paint the rose upon the face
Of the sweet blossoms of our race,
And give unto the youthful vow
The gentle eye, and earnest brow;
That dip the flowers in every dye,
Shed by the day-king passing by;
That scatter on the breezy swell
The spring and summer's fragrant smell;
And on the autumn's fullness paint
The dreams of many a raptured saint!
That teach the bee, with honeyed lip,
The dew distilled in flowers to sip;
That fly upon the eagle's wing,
And teach the skylark how to sing;

9

That travel on the lightning's flash,
And revel in the thunder's crash ;
That sing through all the starry night,
And bring the sun's first beams of light ;
That send the cloudy, fleecy shade,
To temper noon's hot fierceness made,
And shake the liquid drops around
Upon the waiting, thirsty ground ;
Making the rivers overflow,
And buried seeds to sprout and grow ;
That on the wingéd south winds rove,
Clothing with life the naked grove ;
That scatter beauty's light below
The waves, that deep and darkling flow ;
That stand upon the mountain's height,
And open to man's wondering sight
Alternate beauties, far and nigh,
Upon the earth, and in the sky !
And when on earth's illumined zone
The sun declines, beckon him home ; —
Beckon him home, where Love's soft eye
Smileth to see his footsteps nigh ;
Beckon him home, where children cling
Around her neck who makes them sing ;
Where gentle words are passing round
From lip to lip, where love is found ;
Where Silence smiles serene and bright,
Blessing each happy inmate's sight ;
Where modest Sympathy is nigh,
To ease the toil, and check the sigh ;

And when dread Sorrow enters there,
To wipe the heavy falling tear ;
Where Innocence doth softly sleep,
And Sympathy doth often weep ;
Where Death has been, but left a trace,
On every heart of the dear face ;
Where words are spoken, soft and low,
Of those who sleep, where all must go ;
Where absent ones seem to draw near,
In Memory's blesséd evening cheer,
And in the social, swelling song,
Their once loved strains still float along!
Where Hope springs up in every breast,
And whispers of the coming rest ;
Where absent ones shall all abide,
Close to each loving, dear one's side ;
Where love is bound not, but shall be
Like ocean's waters, — full and free !
Bring us, thou wingéd seraphim,
One strain from your o'erflowing hymn ;
And on it bid our spirits rise,
With thee, to view thy paradise !
How sad the spirit, when have fled
Thy dreams from the poor aching head !
But, full of hope and joy, is found
The heart that listens to the sound !
O Ocean ! let thy anthems roll
The song of praise into my soul !
And when thy waves are lifted high,
Bid thou my wildest raptures fly !

And thou, O Earth! prolong the strain,
And let thy winds declare His name,
Who hangs thee in the boundless sky,
There in tremendous speed to fly
Around thy central orb of light,
In ceaseless order, in His sight!
When the wild winds and waters rest,
In the sweet moonlight may my breast
Be filled with softer songs of praise
To Him whose glory round me plays
In evening's concave, where I see
Some glimpses of Infinity!
O, wondrous Night! I here behold
Those lights that to my eyes unfold
His outside glory, who doth fill
The distant, deep, invisible!
And yet He deigns to dwell below,
In the poor glowworm's mimic glow;
And the small firefly shines as bright
As Venus, in her distant flight,
To Him who filleth all their fires
With His own glory; and desires
All things created thus to shine,
In their own nature, all divine!
And gives to all, on every zone,
A proper place, a pleasant home.
Sweet Home of Love! dear sacred spot!
To whom shall fall that happy lot,
He need not envy pampered pride,
While Love sits smiling at his side:

He need not court the monarch's smile,
Whose heart receives the holy oil
Of sweet affection ; life to him
Is like the voice of seraphim,
That sings forever ! like the sound
Of bubbling fountains under ground.
He need not seek the vulgar crowd,
Where profanation, rank and loud,
Offends the ear ; but silence, sweet,
Floats round him, where the fond ones meet :
He needs no draught from Lethe's bowl
To drown the passions of the soul ;
But like the cloud that floats along,
Scatters his gems of love and song, —
Refreshing hearts, that taint of sin
Hath crushed, and left them sorrowing.
He walks like Mary's Son of old,
Turning earth's desert sands to gold ;
And oft like Him, he weeps to know
That sin and sorrow reign below ;
Like Him, he gives his life to bless,
With living green, this wilderness.
O, sorrowing World ! one soul like this
Is like a constant stream of bliss,
Flowing and murmuring down thy plains
In dulcet tones of heaven's own strains !
One home of love on earth's sad face,
Shall glad the annals of a race !
O for a Nation filled with love !
One favored Nation placed above

Dark hate, and scorn, and selfish lust ;
With motives high above the dust ;
With human wants and human right,
Flaunted aloft in living light,
From every banner, on each dome !
Heaven's winds shall whisper, " This is Home ! "

———◆◆———

PART I.

1. I've wandered far, o'er land and sea,
   From scenes and friendships dear to me,
   And sought for wealth in honest toil,
   'Mid busy din, and the turmoil
   Of crowded cities, — crowded full
   Of wealth and commerce : wit and fool
   Together mingle in the mart,
   Fast friends, — while gold doth bind the heart.

2. I've dwelt amid the rural cots
   In dimpled valleys ; lovely spots,
   Where Nature smileth evermore,
   And giveth forth her golden store
   To brawny arms and simple hearts,
   That know not of the wily arts
   Of Fashion, and its devotee,
   And only native beauty see !

3. I've worshipped 'neath the aged oak ;
Joined the wild, solemn dirge which broke
The silence of the Sabbath air ;
And laid to rest the form, as fair
As lilies growing in the glade,
Where she had lived, and loved, and prayed ;
And sadly shed the parting tear,
Mingled with wild flowers on her bier !

4. I've brushed away the early dew,
Up where the mountain eagle flew ;
And watched in his majestic way
The gorgeous Monarch of the Day ;
Drank of the limpid mountain spring,
Up where the birds their matins sing ;
And viewed the smiling lowlands, spread
As lovely as an angel's bed !

5. I've floated on the Hudson's breast,
When, like a maiden it was drest
In wild flowers ; and with flowing hair,
Drooped on its banks the willow fair ;
The swallow kissed its dimpled face,
And swiftly passing, left a trace
Of blushing beauty, when the sun
His watchful course had almost run.

6. And when its waters calm did sleep,
And the soft moon looked down so deep
Into its silent, throbbing heart,
It sometimes seemed to dream, and start

With sudden motion, as the breeze
Crept stealthily among the trees;
Like lovely Lucrece, when the door
Admitted Tarquin to her floor! [1]

7. Sleep on, sweet Hudson! Thou shalt be
   A bright, pure virgin stream, when she
   And the fond poet cease to thrill
   The human heart; — thou, thou shalt still
   Flow on as placid then as now,
   And nightly stars shall deck thy brow,
   And the moon, smiling, tell to thee
   The lover's vow of constancy!

8. I've seen the forkéd lightning play, ·
   In flashing beauty, far away;
   Leaving its thunders rolling on
   The mountain tops, when it had gone
   To other lands; like bolt of Jove,
   Flaming in terror; — still to rove
   Forever, round earth's circled zone,
   While her eternal course shall run!

9. Fair Hudson, thou art beauty's queen!
   Adown thy living banks is seen
   The fisher's cot, in humble guise,
   And on thy sloping lawns arise
   The rural palace, like a gem
   Sparkling in Nature's diadem!
   And, built back in the ancient time,
   The pointing spire, and house divine;

And all around its walls are spread
The crumbling emblems of the dead ;
For Time moves on, and with his tooth
Eats out the words of love and truth ;
And they who bathed them with their tears
Sleep calm and still, beneath the years !

10. How snug and sweet the village home,
    Where kindred's purest ties have grown !
    How lazily the smoke ascends
    Amid the branching tree, that bends
    Above the roof, where children sing,
    Whose grandsires set the acorn in !
    Let Goldsmith sing sweet Auburn's praise,
    In other lands, in other days ;
    But in thy lovely vales are found —
    Scarce equalled in the wide world round —
    Sweet, quiet villages, that lie,
    The fairest pearls beneath the sky !

11. Thy Palisades, a fluted wall,
    Breaking the sunny rays that fall,
    In rippled silver, on thy breast, —
    Like some Plutonian city's crest,
    Thrown up in a convulsive throb,
    In spite, or sport, of that fierce God, —
    Stand out in beauty, full of grace,
    To decorate thy lovely face ;
    While mount on mount, and hill on hill,
    Build up thy cloud-capped Katerskill !

2

12. How graceful, on thy yielding breast,
     Our floating palaces ! all drest
     In playful streamers, in the breeze ;
     And playful hearts, in joyous ease ;
     And maidens fair, and lovers gay,
     Dancing away the summer day
     To music sweet ; while joyous mirth
     Brings paradise to this fair earth !

13. Adown thy ever-placid stream
     Flow wealth and commerce, like a dream
     In fancy bred ! Old Egypt's pride, —
     Fair Nilus, — on her boasted tide,
     Saw not thy grandeur ere she fell
     Beneath the tyrant's withering spell ;
     Yet in thy youth I sing of thee, —
     What shalt thou in the ages be ?

14. Sing, O my Muse, the coming time !
     Sing of the grapes when turned to wine !
     Sing of the cradle passed away !
     Of starlight, lost in opening day !
     Of spring time, lost in summer flowers !
     Of summer, lost in clustered bowers,
     Waiting the wine press ! Sing, O, sing
     Of eaglets mounted on the wing,
     And looking from the distant skies,
     Back where their nest so humble lies.

15. Sing of our Hudson, when old Time
     Hath brought another century's chime !

When solitudes are peopled towns,
And millions fill the village rounds;
When man and woman both shall be
Nurtured in love and liberty;
When every soul shall claim its own,
And Justice give to all a home!

16. Then shall thy waters gladly flow
To the old Ocean, down below,
And whisper in his aged ear
The secrets of the fond hearts near; —
And he shall clap his hands in glee!
And on the west wind's ecstasy,
His joy in thunder tones shall roll
To every freedom-loving soul!

17. I've sauntered down thy pebbly stream,
O Juniata! and my dream
Was of the noblest Indian chief,
His pride, his glory, and his grief.
'Twas here the haughty native roved,
And in thy waves the maid he loved
Bathed her lithe limbs, and in thy face
Viewed the last Queen of all her race:
And thus I seemed to hear her sing,
In tones as sweet as the carolling
Of the mocking-bird, that listened near,
These words, which fell upon my ear: —

18. "Come, maidens, come to the river's banks,
And sing with me of the storied ranks

Of warriors brave, in the olden time,
With tomahawks bright from the distant mine;
In countless crowds, like the forest leaves,
With colors bright[2] as the spirit weaves,
When his voice is hushed, and silence sings
Her songs of peace on the red-bird's wings!

19. " Come, sing with me of the mingled chiefs,
While they passed around the pipe of peace;
Of the passionate voice,[3] that filled each soul,
(Like the lowering clouds that flash and roll!
With terrible fear ;) like the voice of death,
When the youthful warrior yields his breath!
Though absent and silent, yet they roam
In happiness in the spirit home.

20. " They've passed away, but they wander free
Where the maidens' hearts are full of glee;
Where the darting game is ever seen,
And the arrows speed in flashing sheen;
And the pluméd wings their brows adorn;
And age shall not waste the manly form;
Where the faithful dog is ever nigh,
Still watching to catch his master's eye.

21. " And the pale face hath not entered there
To fell the trees, or poison the air
With the blasting fever's [4] loathsome spell,
When friends whisper not the last farewell:
To give them the bowl that maddens the eye
With lust, and Hate's hot passions, that fly

Like arrows of death, till maiden and brave
Have passed in crowds to death and the grave !

22.   " Come, let us be joyful, blithe, and gay !
We know that our tribes are passing away ;
We know that the red men shall not return ;
No more the council-fires shall burn
On the Juniata's craggy banks ;
No more shall be seen the circling ranks
Of visiting warriors, gaily plumed,
To notes of revenge and victory tuned !

23.   "But the tribes that hence have passed away,
Are only waiting for those that stay ;
Are only waiting to see them come
To the happy Indian's deathless home !
Where the fleet-footed youths the flowers shall
      bring
That grow in the ever-budding spring
Of the spirit land ; — to the maids who sing
Like the birds that there are carolling ! "

24.   Flow on, clear river ! I would be
As thoughtless of the past as thee ;
But in my heart the mountains lie
Of childhood ; — back to them I fly !
Thine, thine forever round thee tower,
As close as in thy natal hour !
And when in kindred dust I lie,
Shall point man upward to the sky

25. Broad Mississippi! I have been
    Where thy bold rocky banks are seen;
    Presenting to the traveller's eye
    Enchantment, as he passeth by!
    And on thy distant waters viewed —
    (To him with ancient lore imbued,
    Impressing on his mind the walls
    Of Petra, where the sunlight falls

26. In fiercer floods ;) — insculptured heights,
    Strange, wonderful as fairy flights ;
    Columns [5] made by the mighty hand
    Of Him who built the ocean strand ;
    Laughing to scorn man's labored shrine,
    That crumbles 'neath the wheels of Time ;
    Teaching to man, on every stone,
    How transient every earthly home !

27. I've seen the marshes, wide and low,
    Through which thy tributaries flow, —
    Yielding the golden-colored grain,[6]
    That waves in beauty on each plain ;
    Waves rank and tall, beyond compare
    In northern climes ; where purer air
    Giveth to man a better boon,
    When north winds sing their winter tune.

28. Thy lofty heights, where Vicksburg towers,
    Are peaceful now as smiling bowers ;
    But yesterday those heights were filled
    With Treason's whelps, whose engines killed

The sons of Liberty, and fed
Thy waters with her youthful dead ! —
Ah, let them sleep ! the young and brave,
Forever, 'neath thy yellow wave !

29. But 'twas not long, for Treason fell
At sound of Freedom's natal bell ! [7]
And when her Eagle noised it round,
The foemen's tracks were only found
Receding from the generous stream,
Leaving alone the horrid dream,
A troubled nightmare of the past,
Where tyrants' cursèd hosts are cast !

30. Fair, smiling Peace ! forever dwell
Where those great waters flow and swell ;
Let peaceful millions line each shore,
And every tributary pour
Its varied products to the marts
That send them to the distant parts
On wings of commerce, blessing all
The homes built on the earth's wide ball !

31. Thou unborn Future ! oft we sigh
To pierce thee with the prophet's eye !
To view thy conquests in the land
Favored by Nature's lavish hand.
All climes are here — from icy death,
To the fierce summer's hottest breath ;
Thy northern sons vex wintry mines,
While thy long southern summer shines —

32.   Ripening the richest fruits of earth ;
      And pluméd warblers issue forth,
      With gushing rapture, on each tree,
      Swelling the song of praise. — To Thee,
      O Father ! all things living tend
      To swell that song that ne'er shall end ;
      And most of all, Thy praise is shown,
      Where man hath found a happy Home.

33.   How sweet the moonbeams gently rest
      At midnight on thy yielding breast,
      In rippled silver, soft and light,
      Playing like childhood, in the sight
      Of the maternal love, whose eye
      Alone can see the gems that lie
      In the young spirit, through the face
      That makes her home a happy place !

34.   Well, let your orange blossoms blow ;
      Let man, for lucre eager, go
      To pluck the fruits ; let fleecy flowers [8]
      Tempt Mammon from ancestral bowers ;
      Let Commerce, with her countless sails,
      Seek wealth amid the southern gales ;
      But let me dwell in the mild zone
      That bounds my blesséd native Home !

Home is home, though poor and rude ;
Home is more than house and food :

Home can never be expressed,
Till the soul has found its rest.
Home is transient here below,
And its term we cannot know :
It is like the sun's last ray,
Dying with departing day.
Home is like the robin's nest,
Now in downy feathers drest,
But to-morrow nowhere found,
In the air or on the ground.
Home is like the ship at sea,
Sailing on eternally ;
Oft the anchor forth we cast,
But can never make it fast.
Home is like the bluebird's wing
Fluttering in the breath of spring,
Seeking for some quiet nook,
Near the pebbly, purling brook.
Home is never rounded out ;
There's always fear, always doubt.
Joy is short, but sorrow long,
And groans are heard in every song.
Home is sweet when love is there,
Breathing perfume on the air !
And the fairest flowers below,
Underneath Love's sunshine grow !
Home is like the ocean deep,
Where the fairest treasures sleep ;
Brightest gems lie sparkling there,
Pearls and rubies, rich and rare !

Pearls of purity and grace,
Dwell within the sacred place !
Ruby love, of ruddy hue,
Courses every veinlet through !
Like a stream Love's waters flow ;
Or like Morning's fairest glow.
And Love's streamlets ever come
Back to rest in Love's own Home !

————•••————

PART II.

35. WINDING Ohio ! thou art set
Where hostile armies oft have met,
And Freedom trembled on the beam
Where thy unceasing waves are seen :
Oppression could not hedge thy tide
While Freedom smiled on yonder side ; [9]
Smiled like a Goddess ! bidding come
The panting bondman to her home !

36. Rejoice, O River ! Let thy waves
Roll their glad music in thy caves ;
And on thy spreading sycamore,
Let the wild eagle boasting pour
His screaming, daring notes abroad !
While humbler warblers on the sod

Take up his notes in softer strains,
For on each shore glad Freedom reigns !

37. Upon thy smiling banks are seen
The dense, dark cedars, ever green,
Bending their matted branches low,
Inviting Winter's purest snow
To form a lovely robe of white
Upon the mountain's towering height,
And nestling round the cottage door,
Like friendship, constant, fadeless, pure.

38. And the sweet apple-blossoms blow
In beauty where thy waters flow,
Flinging their odors on the breeze,
When youthful Spring invades the trees ;
And the gay peach-blows cluster there,
Offering to the industrious care
Of the sweet insect honeyed store,
Till his filled labyrinth runneth o'er.

39. The cornfield spreadeth down thy plains,
Long, low, and wide, while Summer reigns,
Maturing 'neath the sun's hot rays,
And quaffing in the dew, that plays
Among its long, extending leaves,
While midnight, in her cunning, weaves
The gentle drops that slowly sink
Into the stalk, that it may drink.

40. Then the rich, yellow grains appear,
In the long Autumn of the year,
Promising food when north winds blow,
And the old Ice King reigns below !
And the ripe fruit divides the care
Of the glad husbandmen, who share
With beast and fowl abundant gains,
And Plenty in the cottage reigns.

41. Thy wood-clad mountains smiling stand,
Inviting man's industrious hand
To vex their sides, and take away
The food [10] that makes the engines play
Upon the broad-faced stream below,
Making the rapid commerce flow
From north to south, from east to west,
Till every clime is amply blest ; —

42. Inviting man to fell the trees,
And every passing eye to please
With fruit, and flower, and lowing kine,
And fleecy flocks ; till coming time
Presents the pleasing, wondrous change,
In all the vast, extended range [11]
Of the old River ; — thickly strewn —
Millions, who sing the Song of Home !

43. I've floated on thy tranquil breast,
In the sweet Sabbath's quiet rest,
And wondered — when the years roll by —
If Memory's speedy wings shall fly

Back to the scenes that charmed me then,
And paint upon my straining ken
Thy gorgeous sunsets,[12] calm and grand,
Inviting to the spirit land ! —

44. Wondered if Time's swift, silent feet
Shall spare my fading eyes, to meet
The pleasing views that spread around,
The mossy bank, the grassy mound ;
The nestling cot, the sacred dome ;
The hanging rock, lofty and lone ;
The busy hands forming each stone
To grace some neighboring City Home ; —

45. The moving craft, that up and down,
Look like some floating, busy town,
Greeting, with an unearthly scream,
Each other with the voice of steam ;
Bearing their living freight, to rest
In the wild silence of the West ;
Or bringing fond ones, eager, prone,
To rest in the old Eastern Home ! —

46. Wondered if, on some boat's high deck,
Gazing on some projecting wreck,
My thoughts shall bring the pleasant time,
When on thy waves those friends of mine
Were bland and free, anxious to see
The changing scenes, pointing to me
Nature and Art, in pleasing view,
In tones of friendship, kind and true ; —

47.　Wondered if, on the wide expanse
　　　Of the old Ocean, I might chance
　　　To taste its briny, liquid flow,
　　　And think of crystals,[13] white as snow,
　　　Distilled from thy deep well-springs there,
　　　Where rising flames invade the air
　　　Like fiery mountains, day and night,
　　　Dispensing far a beacon light !

48.　But all Earth's pleasures pass away,
　　　Like the last lingering purple ray
　　　Of Evening's glory.　O, how soon
　　　The smile of love is lost in gloom !
　　　And when the pulse of hope beats high,
　　　Its cherished objects quickly fly ;
　　　And like a solemn, funeral knell,
　　　Sounds the fond, parting word — Farewell !

———◦◦◦———

　　　Soft and low, sad and sweet,
　　　Glide away friendly feet ;
　　　Soft and sweet greetings fall
　　　Where Love's words fondly call.
　　　Sadness reigns when we see
　　　Fond ones fade, droop, and flee ;
　　　Tenderest, dearest, saddest spell,
　　　When we say — Fare ye well !

　　　Press them close, hold them fast ; —
　　　It may be quite the last

Look of love, word of love —
In the bower, in the grove !
Listen deep, listen still,
Let thy ear take its fill ;
Deeply drink, it is well,
Ere thou say'st — Fare thee well !

Sun's first rays drink the dew ;
Young Love smiles, bright and true ;
Childhood smiles, sweet and fair,
Without guile, without care ;
Friendship true, friendship sweet,
Dwells in hearts warm and deep ;
None can know, none can tell
Who shall first bid — Farewell !

Lovers young, lovers gay,
Quickly fade, pass away ;
Eyes of love, life and light,
Fade away from our sight;
What is life ?   What are we ?
And, alas ! what shall we be ?
Who can guess, who can tell,
After we have said — Farewell ?

Mystery dark, mystery deep !
Like a God, fast asleep,
Slumbers on, evermore ;
While we cry, o'er and o'er —
" Wake, O, wake !   We would be
Taught of thee, O Mystery ! "

Still he sleeps, and Time's bell
Swings and tolls — "Fare thee well!"

Work and wait, work and sing;
Work without, work within.
All things change ; nought can die !
Work for all, work to-day ;
Pray and work, work and pray.
The result old Time shall tell,
After thou hast said — Farewell.

Dearest souls, fondest friends,
Never die ! Life but ends,
Like the day, soon to rise
Glorious in the eastern skies !
Cheer up, heart ! sing away !
Midnight is approaching day !
And the last, sad, feeble groan
Ushers in the Endless Home !

PART III.

49. Dear Childhood's Home ! I cannot see
One spot, upon the land or sea,
So bright, so beautiful, so free,
So sweet, so full of love, as thee !
Thy hill-sides drink a purer dew,
And from their tops my eyes would view

The loveliest stream that ever lay
'Mid flowers, to tempt the God of Day!

50. I doubt not that the Grecian band
Shed tears, when on the distant strand
Of the old sea, that washed their land,[14]
And shouting, clasped each other's hand!
Shed tears which danger could not draw;
Which circling foemen never saw;
Shed only o'er the sleeping bravo
At midnight, when around his grave!

51. O, why doth Nature bind so fast
The soul of man to the young past?
Make him a child when Memory brings
Young life upon her golden wings?
And why doth Fortune's brightest hour,
Still paint, with a resistless power,
The holiest star in heaven's wide dome,
A beacon to his Native Home!?

52. The bitterest cup of Sorrow's night
Grows sweeter by the blesséd light
Of other days; but sad and dark
The wanderer's lot, if on his heart
There cometh not his mother's kiss,
His father's smile. O! give him this
When sorrow clings, and dangers come;
Then he can smile, and think of Home!

53. Ah ! sadly have I viewed the grave
    Of him who crossed the distant wave ;
    And wondered if the dying groan
    Was hushed when visions came of home !
    Like the chafed spirit on the rock,
    Who, dying, heard the battle's shock ;
    And in the gorgeous, filmy trance,
    Cheered on the warrior sons of France !

54. He could not die an exile there, —
    He who the cannon's mouth could dare, —
    He could not die until his dream
    Brought back his lovely Josephine ;
    And in her eye beholdeth he
    The flower of Gallic chivalry !
    Prophetic chieftain,[15] every bone
    Shall rest in thy Adopted Home !

55. Sweet child of Israel's later years, —
    Child of his Rachel, and his tears, —
    Fond prattler to thy brethren's ears,
    Exciting thus their jealous fears ; —
    What gave thee comfort in the pit ?
    What made thee for thy station fit ?
    Thy vision saw the patriarch come,
    To rest in thy Abundant Home !

56. Thou ancient singer, Jesse's son !
    What prompted thee when thou didst run,
    And challenge to the fatal fight
    Yon spearman,[16] in his towering height ?

A lamb unto the lion sent:
What to thy heart, the valor lent
Unequalled, when that small, smooth stone
Entered thy sling?　'Twas God and Home !

57.　And thou, O Jesus ! lovelier still ;
　　　Thou chief of men, through every ill ;
　　　The great Exemplar.　Sad and lone,
　　　Despised, rejected by Thine own ; —
　　　Didst love them still, and walk about
　　　Jerusalem ; still casting out
　　　Their demons ; — Thou didst sadly groan
　　　O'er Lazarus, and his vacant Home !

58.　Thou Holy One, and full of grace ;
　　　Thou purest, tenderest of the race ;
　　　Thou Incarnation of our God !
　　　Homeless Thy weary footsteps trod ;
　　　Thou Medium, binding to the throne
　　　The erring ones by thy sad moan ;
　　　Thou meek, mild Lamb of God, alone,
　-　　Leadest the weary sinner Home !

59.　In thy last hour, a helpless one
　　　Gave to the cross the sweetest son
　　　That ever blest a mother's heart ;
　　　And in that hour thou couldst not part
　　　From her thou lovedst till thou hadst won
　　　For her a sympathizing son ; [17]
　　　Till on her future Thou hadst thrown
　　　A flower, to blossom in her Home !

Sad and weary, pure and holy,
   Fading from the earth away ;
Full of grace, so still and lowly,
   Brightest of the sons of day !
Weeping for the broken-hearted ;
   Giving back the widow's child ;
Shedding tears o'er the departed ;
   Calm, content, and meek, and mild !

Teacher of earth's poor and erring ;
   Sympathizing with their woes ;
Loving all, but none compelling ;
   Weeping o'er thy bitterest foes ;
Wandering in the desert sadly ;
   Poor, and in the tempter's power ;
And where demons torture madly,
   Scattering Love's own precious dower !

Standing on the rugged mountain,
   Where the poor and needy meet ;
Giving them, from Love's own fountain,
   Living waters, pure and sweet !
Still beseeching, never cursing ;
   Lifting up the bruiséd reed ;
And the shorn lambs kindly nursing,
   Binding up the hearts that bleed.

Dropping in the furrowed ages
   Seeds that shall to beauty grow ;
Blossoming on endless pages,
   Flowers of truth, like purest snow !

What to Thee were wealth and station,
  Or the tribute honor brings?
What the homage of a nation,
  Men's applause, or praise of kings?

'Twas alone the Father's blessing
  Could thy heart with rapture fill;
And to Him thy prayer addressing,
  'Mid all pain thy heart was still.
When the world's unholy clamor
  Culminates its loudest din,
Faith descries Truth's pure, white banner,
  Far above the plains of sin.

Thou, O Jesus! still art smiling
  Through the mighty clouds of earth;
While below our feet are toiling,
  Hasting to the spirit birth.
Sing, O sing! ye bright immortals;
  Sing His goodness and His love!
When ye ope for us life's portals,
  We will join your choir above!
Sing, O Earth! the coming glory
  Glimmers in the eastern sky!
And the coming Christ, so holy,
  Through the vista draweth nigh!

PART IV.

60. Home, sweetest music to the ear!
     Its cadence doth the pathway cheer
     'Mid deserts, where the hot sands burn
     The traveler's feet.   There he doth turn
     His longing eyes to the old scenes,
     And sleeping, fondly in his dreams
     Drinks from the trickling mountain spring,
     And hears the song his loved ones sing!

61. And in the city's busy throng,
     Its mirth, its revelry, and song,
     Its dissipation and its cant,
     'Mid all its flowers, a foreign plant,
     He bloometh not, till Friendship find
     A sympathetic, kindred mind;
     Till this within his heart doth bloom,
     His spirit sighs for love and Home!

62. Hail, magic charm! fond Childhood's bliss!
     The father's smile, the mother's kiss;
     The brother's laugh, the sister's love;
     The new life, cooing like a dove;
     The present of the painted toy,
     That fills the little cup with joy; —
     Here, in the budding soul, is sown
     The seed that groweth up to Home!

63. Then happy school days coming on,
  When buds have into blossoms grown,
  How proudly doth the satchel gay,
  When goeth he to school away,
  Hang on his arm! As proud as shield
  On warrior's arm in tented field!
  And soon he tireth, and is prone
  To seek his supper and his Home.

64. Then Manhood, with its dreams and hopes,
  Painteth to him a day that opes
  In splendor; brightly luring on
  The dreamer; passing, one by one,
  The enchanting projects, till the day
  Is lengthened, and they've passed away!
  Then weary, sad, dejected, lone;
  He thinketh of the good old Home!

65. Then hoary age, the resting-time,
  Cometh apace; and he doth pine
  For good and true ones gone to rest,
  Leaving the weary one; who pressed,
  So often, in the days gone by,
  The gentle forms, which oft did lie
  Upon his breast. I've heard thee groan,
  O Age! and vainly sigh for Home!

66. Is this the sum of human life?
  The changing passions and their strife?
  The anxious struggles, ceasing not,
  Through all the human, common lot?

The toilsome haste, the tasteless goal,
That satisfieth not the soul?
Earth hath not, on her lengthened zone,
One constant, happy, changeless Home!

67. Author of life, birth, youth, and age;
Of Nature, filling every page
With motion, constant change, decay;
Hope in its birth, like opening day;
Joy in its youth, that swelling joy!
O! why should Time its bliss destroy?
In age 'tis past; ambition high,
Filleth the fond, aspiring eye; —

68. Through all, kind Nature leadeth on
Her children, till the race is run;
Leadeth them on to Thee: to Thee,
O Father! every flower I see
Blossoms to Thee! and I would bloom
In fragrance, for the living boon;
Scattering the odor of thy love
On others, leading them above; —

69. Above, beyond Earth's passing show;
Its pleasures, coming but to go
More quickly; like the painted fly,
Maturing long, quickly to die;
Above the miser's grasping care,
Who keepeth back the brother's share,
And heapeth up the yellow dust,
Till he becomes a thing accurst!

70. Earth yieldeth, from her swelling breast,
 Abundance ; and her sons are blest
 With roots, and herbs, and crystal spring ;
 With flower, and shrub, and birds that sing ;
 With spreading tree, and verdant sod ;
 With mountains, pointing up to God ;
 With oceans, bearing to each shore
 Their precious burdens evermore !

71. When, like the ocean, shall each soul
 Be freighted for the common whole ?
 When shall each generous impulse flow
 To other hearts, till each shall grow
 In other's welfare ; running on
 In harmony, and all be one ?
 Till then the God within shall sleep,
 And the great brotherhood shall weep ; —

72. Till then shall vainly, meanly rise
 Man's hateful incense to the skies !
 Angels shall weep, and fly above
 To regions where the air is love !
 Up where the miser dwelleth not ;
 Where all have but one common lot,
 One common joy ! O, bring us this,
 Ye spirits, from the realms of bliss !

73. Till this, sweet Bethlehem's song in vain
 Gave man the noblest, sweetest strain
 That ear hath heard, or choir hath sung !
 Thou loving Jesus ! then shall come

Thy Father's kingdom on the earth,
And man obtain his second birth !
Then war shall cease, and discord then
Forsake the happy homes of men.

74. Then Justice shall forsake the rod,
And man shall do the will of God ;
Men after idols shall not stray,
But walk forever in the way
Of justice, peace, contentment sweet,
And equal, men together meet
Around the hearth, around the throne
Of God, and earth shall be a Home !

There's a voice in the breeze when the storm has
      passed by,
And it speaks to the soul in a murmuring sigh !
'Tis mingled with notes of the orphan's sad moan,
And the widow's refrain hath a tear and a groan !

There's a centuried oak, which the firebolt hath
      torn,
And his glory hath fled on the wings of the
      storm ;
And the green fruit lies low 'neath the hurricane's
      breath ;
And beauty lies still in the silence of death !

There's a story of old, that the tyrant hath writ ;
And the raven and owl o'er the past ages flit :
And woman's sad tear, and the patriot's blood,
Rise an incense, and call for the justice of God !

There's an inner light shines in the spirit so deep,
Like the star that burns on, while the lower world
    sleep !
It shall never grow dim till the morning appears,
And fair Justice looms forth in the fullness of years !

And the time hastens on when love's flowers shall
    bloom,
Like the spirit that smiles o'er the sepulcher's gloom ;
And all hearts shall be glad when the sunlight falls
    through,
With its outspreading heaven opened full on the
    view !

Then the nations shall rise, like the birds in the
    spring,
And the wide world shall chorus the songs that they
    sing !
Then Passion shall sleep in the silence of death,
And Virtue shall breathe in the rose's sweet breath !
Then Beauty shall sparkle in every glad eye,
And each spirit shall feel that a brother is nigh ;
Then the life-drops shall flow through each pulsating
    vein,
Like the music of love in its merriest strain !

O ! 'tis coming, 'tis coming ! I hear the bells ring!
It comes like swift love on the carrier dove's wing !
The good time is coming, and soon we shall see
Its waves rolling on, like an infinite sea !

PART V.

75. SAGES and prophets, men of thought,
By whom the Holy Spirit wrought
Wonders of old, wept bitter tears,
Fasted and prayed through lingering years
In poverty, hatred, and scorn ;
Despised, imprisoned, and forlorn ;
Mournful, and sad, dejected, lone ;
Earth's truest children had no home.

76. The men who reared each lofty tower
Were slaves, compelled by men of power
To drag their weary limbs, and bear
The burdens. Wealth has everywhere
Bound down, held firmly down, in chains
The millions ; hoarding up its gains
To still oppress them. Hath it not,
In the long by-gone, been the blot —

77. Of ages ? Hath it not bound down
The common mind ? Doth it not frown

Upon its victim, vaunting still
The power of wealth to bind the will
In chains of fashion? stronger far
On sons of poverty than are
The ties of kindred? froth and foam
Usurp, where else might be a Home.

78. O, simple Truth! how seldom seen
Thy star, where wealth and pride have been!
O, smiling Love! still dwellest thou
Upon the unassuming brow
Of sweet contentment, where the soul
Seeketh a higher, better goal
Than imitation's servile lot, —
For love makes home in lowly cot.

79. Princes and slaves that boon have sought
In Luxury's surfeit, which hath brought
Disease, and pain, and lingering death;
In servile fawning, which hath left
The narrow soul a slave to sin;
High thoughts and aims cannot come in
The heart when man a slave hath grown; —
Such live and die without a Home.

80. Proud Caius, battling for his land,
Beat back the Volscians, and his hand
Brought victory; peace and plenty reigned;
But envy baited, till he stained
His honor, and he fled away
From those he loved, to those who slay

His kindred. O, how fierce the ire !
'Tis like resistless, flaming fire, —

81. When kindred light the torch of hate,
Grow mad, and tempt the dregs of fate :
Brother with brother strives for blood,
Forgetting country, home, and God ;
Bringing afresh the mother's pains,
And covering honor o'er with stains :
Thou, noble Roman,[18] didst become
Its victim, losing life and home !

82. Sad exiles wander through the earth,
Longing for lands that gave them birth;
Pride, poverty, and stubborn will
Holding them back, 'mid every ill ;
While smiling hope covers the dart
That enters many a broken heart ; —
Broken and sad, because alone,
Far distant from the happy home !

83. Thou rugged Alps ! thou land of Tell !
Thy mountain sons remember well
Where beauty, love, and freedom dwell !
Up where the mountain horn doth swell
Its cheerful echoes, warning back
His brothers to the chamois track ;
And though thy children often roam,
'Tis brief ; for love doth call them home !

84. Sons of the forest! ye have fled
    The graves of your ancestral dead;
    Left the grand rivers, on whose banks
    The ancient chiefs surveyed the ranks
    Of the young warriors, chafing there
    For battle, chanting the war prayer
    To the Great Spirit! No more shall come
    The red man to his ancient home!

85. Old Niger! I would sing of thee!
    Soon shall thy children roam as free
    As proud Europa's daring sons!
    Free as the native lion runs
    In thy vast forests; and thy throng
    Shall join the universal song
    Of the redeemed   That song shall be
    The God in Man, and all men free!

86. Land of the legend and the loch!
    Of him [19] who all the echoes woke
    Of thy famed hills; sent through the earth
    Thy beauty; gave the noble worth
    Of thy brave sons to every shore;
    Thy glory in the days of yore!
    What bonny Scotsman e'er did roam,
    Who longed not for his native home? —

87. That sings not with his Bobby Burns
    His lovely Mary? While he earns
    His daily pittance, there doth dwell
    Within his heart the tones that swell

Upon the craggy mountain top,
Bagpipe and clarion, till each rock
Is vocal with the sounding joy,
And home is round the whilom boy!

88. Green Erin! I have seen thy son
In distant lands ; with him have sung
The exile's song ; soothed the sad man
With hope, until his soul began
To swell with better thoughts ; till he
Was filled with love for home and thee!
I've sadly read the mournful stone
Where sleeps thy child, far, far from home!

89. O! Island of the Emerald hue!
Well may thy sons, to nature true,
Long for thy hill-sides and thy plains,
Thy meadows and thy flowery lanes,
Thy rivers and enchanting lakes,
Where silence into music breaks,
'Mid rippling murmurs, soft among
The rocks and trees, that swell the song!

90. Why do ye roam, O, favored race!
To distant lands, from such a place?
Can ye not live where God is seen,
On every hand, in living green?
Where brightness smiles in every eye,
And loving friends are ever nigh?
Hath Fate's relentless fiat sown
The seeds of exile in your home?

91.　Ah, bootless hate ! [20]　O, pious fraud !
　　Dear native land and loving God
　　Are made obscure by Passion's ire,
　　And seen a fierce, consuming fire !
　　O Father, send thy spirit there,
　　And thy poor suffering children spare ;
　　Let peace and love, at thy command,
　　Rejuvenate that lovely land !

O Prophet ! rise, And fix thy eyes
On the towers of the coming paradise !
The day is near, — 'Tis almost here, —
When Truth, like a beacon star, shall appear !

Ashes of Rome, On the Tiber strewn,
Ye are not lost on the salt sea foam ; —
The phœnix shall rise, Where the ember lies,
And thy glory shall come when the darkness dies.

Thy heroes still, Through every ill,
Look down in their love, on each classical hill ;
Thy sun shall yet come, From the ocean foam,
And thy children shall sing in the chorus of Home !

The exile shall rest, When the Star of the West
Hath inspired every land with her beautiful crest ;
When her glory shall be, That the nations are free,
And one flag floats supreme over every sea !

Then mountain and vale, Shall fling on the gale
The love of their sons, on each far-freighted sail ;

4

Then one song shall burst forth, On the wide spread-
    ing earth,
And all lands be one home, for Humanity's birth !

Then faith shall be one, And every son
Shall find the same heaven when his day's work is
    done ;
Then Commerce shall bring, Precious wealth on his
    wing,
And the tidings of love on all people shall fling !

Then every groan, And every moan,
And every jar that the demon hath strown,
And every stone, That Hatred hath thrown,
Shall be lost, and forgot, in the grand song of Home !

PART VI.

92.   "O for a Muse of fire" ! to sing,
    Bold Albion ! of the men who spring
    From thy glad hills and valleys green ;
    Where Science, with her wand hath been,
    Transforming crudeness into form,
    And Commerce filleth Plenty's horn ;
    Where barrens into gardens grow,
    And Eden's beauty dwells below !

93   O, lovely land of shrubs and flowers ;
Of friendly words, and shady bowers ;
Of alternations, strangely new,
That break upon the traveler's view ;
Of peaceful streams, that ever flow
Where the encircling willows grow ;
Where giant elms, that spread around
Their branches, o'er the grassy ground,
Invite the happy flocks to meet
Beneath their shade, and sweetly sleep.

94.   Of oaks, that spread their brawny arms,
Long, large, and rough, but clothed in charms
Of richest verdure, dense and deep,
Inviting summer winds to creep
In gentle dalliance ; whispering low
The gentle tales they hear below ;
While guardian angels linger round,
To wing to heaven love's blissful sound !

95.   O ! 'tis not in the city's din
The angels hear the sacred hymn
Of constant peace ; incessant toil
Makes Passion's fever seethe and boil ;
Fatigue and sorrow smoulder there,
Twin sisters, in the murky air ;
There e'en improvements oft oppress
The poor, and make their comforts less.

96.   Ye ardent lovers of your race,
Bring into every busy place

Where man resides, all that ye can
Of Nature's grace, in every plan ;
Make wide the streets, extend the ground,
Let fruit, and shrub, and flower be found ;
'Tis these that make, wherever strewn,
For man the loveliest, happiest home !

97. Ye gentle flowers, of every hue,
That drink refreshing, nightly dew,
When the bright sun hath passed away,
Until his morning glories play
Upon the hills, along the vales,
And on the merry flapping sails,
Come, fill our homes with your sweet sighs,
And bid us dream of Paradise !

98. O England ! every path I tread,
Where'er my wandering feet are led,
And every bank, on every side,
And every flowing, limpid tide,
And every ancient mossy tower,
Are blest with many a fragrant flower !
He who hath made thy mild, sweet air,
Hath planted seeds of beauty there !

99. Thy ample parks stretch far and wide,
With vale and hill on every side ;
While shaded lakes and copses green
Together dwell, and oft is seen
The soaring crow, and busy bee
Upon the flower, upon the tree ;

Fit types of those who stroll around,
And those who toil upon the ground.

100. Ancestral glories ! ye are fair
As Fancy's flights ; — beyond compare
In other lands, where earth is young
And man is free, where songs are sung
In youthful glee, bold and sublime,
Painting the happy coming time ; —
But O, where Luxury's flowers are strewn,
There's room for many a happy home !

101. O, favored land ! thy balmy air
Gives man the rosy cheek, the fair,
Smooth, soft, white skin, the rotund form,
The jocund welcome, rough and warm ;
The smile of calm content and love
Peeps from each cot, where'er we rove ;
Beams in each eye where Friendship dwells,
And leaps with joy where Music swells !

102. Yes, Music ! thou art native here !
The very earth is full of cheer !
The fleecy flocks, the lowing kine,
Sing through the long, mild summer time ;
The cheerful lark mounts up in glee,
And trembles in his ecstasy !
And where the sparkling brooklet glides,
The chirping bird her children hides.

103. The speckled thrush, in lofty state,
 Pours his loud song to listening mate ;
 And when the day departs, we hear
 The nightingale's sweet, lonely cheer,
 Giving the moon and starry train
 A joyous, welcome, loving strain ;
 And adding to the lover's plea
 The eloquence of minstrelsy !

104. Thou " stone set in the silver sea ; "
 O ! who but one can sing of Thee ?
 Can sing the valor of each son ;
 Of battles fought and victories won ;
 Of Henry's and a Talbot's lance,
 Who scorned the chivalry of France ;
 Can lead us proudly, sadly o'er
 The bloody field of Agincourt : —

105. Can paint to us the gentle Prince,
 Who sweetly pleadeth to convince
 His jailer to be gentle still,
 And do the loving child no ill :
 Plead, Arthur ; let thy innocence
 Banish the tyrant's bribe from thence,
 And soften, with thy prattling tongue,
 The heart, that it shall do no wrong !

106. Thy sons have filled the stranger's grave
 Beyond the distant Indian wave ;
 Left friends and home, that saddest loss,
 To spread the banner of the Cross :

Still straining — when the sun was high —
To distant homes the longing eye !
Nature and duty striving still
Within the mighty, human will.

107. Then to the frigid north they turn,
Upon the polar sea, to learn
The secrets Nature long hath bound
In icy bars, fast bolted round.
O, cruel North King ! give them back [22]
Who wandered o'er thy snowy track :
Fond hearts within thy caverns sleep,
While sad, at home, the loved ones weep !

108. Thy sages lift the curious eye
Up to the boundless evening sky ;
Measure the planets, as they turn
Within their spheres ; and while they burn,
Give laws and bounds, and bid them run
Their shining race around the sun ;
Bring down to earth the milky flood,
And lift the earth up, up to God !

109. What bounds could stop the mad career
Of him who sought the Northern Bear,[23]
And bathed fair Europe in her blood ;
Who worshiped the same loving God !
Burnt the same incense, suffered loss,
In days gone by, for the same cross !
And filled the land his fathers trod
With War's sad, desolating rod ?

110. If thou hadst, at each break of day,
Heard some fond, faithful servant say,
" Thou'rt mortal, creature of the dust ;
Ambition vaunteth now, but must
Soon drop the scepter and the lance,"
Thou proud, adopted son of France !
Thy madness might, in lucid hours,
Have left thee in the happy bowers —

111. Of Home ! beautiful land of flowers !
Fair land of wit and love, which towers
Above all lands in sprightly bliss,
In woman's smiles, in love's wild kiss !
Thy Josephine, that Island dove,
Had filled thy hours with joy and love :
Thy memory might forever burn
In human hearts — man's holiest urn !

112. Who bade the conquering " Fire King " stop,
And chained his eagle to the rock ;
Set bounds to that usurping will,
Amid the waves said, " Peace, be still ; "
Who showed what Freedom's sons could do
On the proud field of Waterloo !
The fearless Lion bared his breast,
And gave earth's homes a peaceful rest !

1 3. Thy Mayflower plowed the western main,[24]
And in its sails the happy train
Of Commerce, Home, and Civil Law
Were wafted, and Columbia saw

The dawning of a brighter day,
Begun when she at anchor lay,
Filled with that thinking, precious freight,
That shapes inevitable fate ! —

114. That embryo Nation, whose broad stride
Hath traversed every ocean tide ;
That Nation that hath luster lent
To every Isle and Continent !
That star of Patriots, giving light
To all who long for human right ;
Bidding each son of toil to come,
And find a freer, wider Home !

———◦◦◦———

Beautiful Isle ! land of the free !
Beautiful song-birds sing unto thee !
Beautiful earth, beautiful sky !
O, why should thy flowers but blossom to die ?

Beautiful bards have sung in thy praise !
Beautiful thoughts thy record shall raise !
Beautiful sons and daughters are thine !
Beautiful souls in thy history shine !

Beautiful deeds thy sons have wrought !
Beautiful things thy wise men have taught !
Beautiful gem in the silver sea —
Beautiful Albion ! I sing of thee.

Beautiful things thy daughters have done!
Beautiful laurels for mercy have won!
Beautiful words of tenderness given!
Beautiful garlands have woven for heaven!

Beautiful groves thy hill-sides adorn!
Beautiful freshness kisses each morn!
Beautiful streamlets murmur away!
Beautiful children adown them play!

Beautiful laws thy pages boast!
Beautiful freedom smiles on thy coast!
Beautiful songs thy children sing!
Beautiful science thy geniuses bring!

Beautiful gardens are blooming around!
Beautiful love in thy homes is found!
Beautiful silence sings on each hill
In beautiful moonlight! so tranquil and still!

When the world lay draped in woe,
    While the Nation's tears fell fast;
When each loving son must go
    At the bugle's clanging blast;

When the widow mourned her dead,
    And her children called in vain
For their scant supply of bread,
    And all hearts were filled with pain;

When the sons of France grew mad
  In the bloody strife of arms;
When all homes, bereft and sad,
  Mourned amid the war's alarms;

When Ambition's favored son
  Rode with pride his prancing steed,
Tramping out life's dying groan,
  Dizzy with the conqueror's meed;

When each nation, sick with blood,
  Pleads the agonizing prayer
To the great All Father God,
  Whose dear love is everywhere, —

Then, O then! dear England came,
  Calm and grand, with measured tread,
'Mid the battle's lurid flame!
  'Mid the dying and the dead:

Came, as once the Spartan band,
  To the willing sacrifice;
There, in danger's pass to stand,
  Where the post of danger lies!

Not in vain thy heroes fell;
  No! the Tyrant's race had run!
Justice calmly said, " 'Tis well!"
  And sweet Peace cried, " It is done!"

Beautiful Mayflower, spread thy sail!
Beautiful sunlight kisses the gale!
Beautiful men, and women fair,
Beautiful prayers are breathing there!

Beautiful hopes sing in each breast!
Beautiful thoughts of coming rest!
Beautiful faith to each is given!
Beautiful trust in God and heaven!

Beautiful hearts those pilgrims bring!
Beautiful birds their welcome sing!
Beautiful was the sea-foam's roar!
Beantiful was the rocky shore!

Beautiful flowers adorn the sod!
Beautiful are the walks they trod!
Beautiful conquests time hath made!
Beautiful where their bones are laid!

Beautiful sing, O coming Time!
Beautiful songs of praise shall be thine!
Beautiful shall all spirits grow!
Beautiful heaven shall reign below!

Beautiful love shall ever increase!
Beautiful hearts shall dwell in peace!
Beautiful Mother! beautiful Son!
Beautiful victories ye have won!!

PART VII.

115. THOU, Western Empire! thou shalt show
.The latent powers that ever grow
In Freedom's light, — on Freedom's soil ; —
Far from the cant and slavish foil
Of hollow pride, and customs slow,
Which bind the human passions low —
Shalt show, on thy untrammeled sod,
Man, in the likeness of his God!

116. O favored Nation, vast and wide!
Extending from Atlantic's tide,
To fair Pacific's golden shore —
Where sing the west winds evermore! —
Where richer mines than Ophir's lie ;
And mountains lift their turrets high
In massive grandeur! where the trees,
Like giants,[25] waving in the breeze
Their sportive limbs : so proudly say
To man, " O, blossom of a day ! "

117. Where wild flowers bloom, in fadeless spring ;
And where the birdlet's tawny wing
Flutters with joy the whole year round !
And where is heard the silvery sound
Of sparkling spray ; where floats above,
Around each hill, with lips of love —

So soft and near ; so close, and sweet ;
Ascending from the mountain's feet
In noiseless steps, to kiss his face ;
Lin—ger—ing long, in close embrace —
The dew-fed cloud ; scarce wooed away
Dissolvent, 'neath the sun's warm ray ! —

118. Where Winter hath not found a place
To show his wrinkled, lifeless face ;
And where the fig-tree's fruits are seen
Luscious and ripe, inmixed with green ; —
Like matron's charms, in ample pride,
With noble offspring at her side ;
And, in her arms the tender bloom,
Love's latest pledge, and light of home !

119. Land of young Hope ! thy wide-spread plains —
Vast solitudes, where silence reigns —
Invite the sons of earth to come
From far and near, and make a home
On Liberty's unequaled soil ;
Where all the sons of honest toil
Are Nature's kings ; but wield no rod
Over the heritage of God !

120. Homes of the Free ! let songs arise
Up to your heroes, in the skies !
Whose unseen forms oft linger round,
Near the dear, natal, holy ground !
To drop the loving, viewless tear ;
And whisper in the loved one's ear

The silent hope, saying, " O, come
Up to the higher, changeless Home ! "

121. They cease not, in their upward flight,
To shed Progression's fadeless light
On the dear land, whose blesséd sod,
In love and sorrow, once they trod ;
For love is changeless in the soul ;
And while eternal ages roll,
The inborn God shall work and plan
The noblest future life for man !

122. O, changeless Love ! man's jeweled crown !
The thoughts of God it bringeth down !
'Tis decked with flowers, and stars, and suns ;
And through the endless ages runs
Its unimpeded, onward march,
Beneath the boundless, royal arch :
Amid the universal dome
It sings : " All space, to me, is Home ! "

123. Dear land of Love ; where Woman's smile
Doth life's most weary hours beguile ;
Where love is free as mountain air,
To bless the youthful, wedded pair ;
Nor birth, nor gold, nor language parts
The nameless bliss of loving hearts ;
But through the lapse of passing years,
They share life's blessings and its tears !

124. Hope of all lands ! thy children see
Fulfillment for each prophecy
Given to man, through every age,
On Inspiration's ample page ;
Here halls of science, opened wide,
Invite the youth, on every side,
To come, and drink the living stream
That flows forever, fresh and green !

125. Yes, knowledge shall exalt the race ;
And virtue flourish in each place
Where truth is free ; goodness shall grow
In hearts that wisdom's precepts know ;
The intellectual eye shines bright,
Where Nature's laws and Nature's light
Are understood, and freely shown ;
These give to man a peerless Home !

126. Joy of all lands, dear loving Home !
Thy sacred halls give man alone
His real life ; — his nest of love,
Where all his passions soar above
Life's isolation and its grave ;
And where, no longer held a slave
To self and lust, his nature springs
To higher aims, and nobler things ; —

127. Thou art his covert from the storm ;
The cradle, where his hopes are born ;
His fount of inspiration, where
Fond, loving objects claim his care ;

The golden band, that binds his heart
To every other precious part
Of that dear round, the Family Tree;
Best emblem of the heaven to be!

128. O, bold Reformer! stay thy hand;
Thou hast a mission, great and grand;
Earth's sorrows, and her wrongs, are thine
To soothe, to banish, and refine; —
Make sharp thy blade for truth and right;
Drown Error in truth's flood of light!
But, O! invade not the bright dome
That bounds man's holiest ties — his Home!

129. Bind fast and strong, mysterious coil, —
Calmly beneath the waves, that boil
On rough Atlantic's troubled breast;
Bind the old East to the young West,
In bands of love and sympathy;
And let all Lands, all Nations, be
The dwellings of the good and free;
One wide expanse of Liberty!

130. Bind fast, strong coil, the giant son, —
While he his upward course shall run
To the old mother; whose proud heart,
Taught his incipient steps to start
On that grand journey, whose high goal
Shall yet expand the human soul,
Far, far beyond the narrow place
Of home and kindred and the race

131. Of man, — one, indivisible,
    Fraternal, universal whole, —
    Shall be one family ; shall know,
    The duties and the cares which flow
    From Brotherhood ; and knowing, do
    The brother's part ; then shall the view
    Of the Omnipotent become
    Well pleased, and Earth shall be a Home !

PART VIII.

132. LAND of the limner, whose grand page,
    Brought Satan, with his mighty rage,
    Through horrid Chaos' monstrous mere,
    Down to the distant, new-made sphere ;
    Where angels saw, with loving eyes,
    The loving pair of Paradise !
    Carried to heaven their daily prayer,
    On snowy wings, through balmy air !

133. Unto thy noble Muse was given
    Bright visions of the plains of heaven !
    Ten thousand harps, of sweetest sound,
    Triumphant swelling ; circling round
    The throne of God, in angel hands ;
    Chanting the songs of warrior bands ;

Making the boundless concave ring,
With peans of heaven's conquering king !

134. O, happy plains ! why should earth be
So far from thence ? and why do ye
O angels ! walk no more with men
In sweet communion, glad, as when ·
The earth was young; and every bower
Of paradise, and every flower
On pristine earth, that bloomed around,
Saw God ; and all was hallowed ground ?

135. Thou, sacred bard, alone couldst bring
The horrid, shameless form of sin
To mortal view ; and thy rough pen,
Alone, could bring to human ken
The mighty, sulphurous thunders, sent
From God, to heaven's high battlement !
And Satan, with his crew, fast prone
To hell, the base usurper's home !

136. Thy Comus ; with enchantment bold,
Shows virtue in a mortal mold ;
And in thy sacred, fond distress,
With thee we weep for Lycidas !
And sad Manoah's son doth fill
The fountain of the human will,
With the soft streams that ever flow,
From human hearts, for human woe !

137. Blind Poet; [26] he who filled thine eyes
With visions fair, of Paradise;
Who led thee, in the desert wild,
With his sad, fasting, holy child;
Who took thee near Siloa's stream;
And opened to thy raptured dream
The sapphire curtain, whence is seen,
The shepherd, 'mid the pastures green —

138. Beside the peaceful, silent flood,
Flowing fast by the throne of God;
Imparted from the solar sphere,
The magic of Ithuriel's spear;
And showed thee, in its golden light,
The false, bad angel in his flight; —
He saw thee in the spirit groan;
Sent Gabriel down, and took thee home!

139. Thou contemplative child of clay,
The pious heart delights in Gray;
And Beaus and Belles of London pray
For the good times of sprightly Gay;
And Armstrong's song is still approved,
By those who Hygeia's laws have loved;
While fancy's flight, and love, are seen,
In Spenser's matchless Fairy Queen!

140. Bold bard, of wit's sharp, comic verse;
No son of song doth yet rehearse,
Like thee, the follies of mankind;
And none, like thee, have sought to find,

The depth of madness, which doth bind
In sacred chains, the human mind ;
Cant still doth need thy flashing blade,
As when a pious Cromwell prayed.

141. Unequaled Butler ! time shall see
Man disinthralled through wit and thee !
For when calm reason pleads in vain,
Thy verse, in a resistless strain,
" Shall laugh mankind to common sense ;
And smiling, Reason's laws dispense : "
Be proud, O Albion ! of thy son ;
No other land hath such an one !

142. Immortal Dreamer ! [27] what to thee
Was earth and all its pageantry ?
What gaoler could the spirit bind,
That the strait, narrow way would find ;
Or keep the anxious Pilgrim back,
Till he had lost the heavy pack ;
Till the sad, weary, burdened soul,
Looked on the Cross, and was made whole !

143. Yes, son of toil ! thy footsteps trod
The narrow path that leads to God,
With constant labor ; and thy way
Was set with snares, from day to day ;
But thy " Great Heart " fought brave for thee,
The sinless land of rest to see !
The land of Beulah, thou hast shown,
Is thine at last, and thou art home !

144. I fain would to the vision ope,
     Of him who reads, the muse of Pope;
     Of Shelley, Byron, and of Moore; —
     Bright sons of genius! whose rich store
     Of fancy, love, and beauty pour
     A flood of glory evermore
     Upon their race, and upon thee,
     Land of the great, the good, and free!

145. All hail! fair land of lofty song!
     I would thy noblest praise prolong;
     Would sing of thine, would sing of thee!
     I, thy sad child, would gladly be
     One of thy favored progeny
     Of wit and song; but none but He,
     Who spake from out dread Sinai's height,
     Can give the bard's transcendent flight!

146. Enough, Great Source, for me,[28] the page
     That singeth of the "Golden Age;"
     That bringeth to the upturned eye,
     The regions where the angels fly!
     That whispereth to the dying saint
     Angelic welcomes, soft and faint,
     But full of glory! for they say,
     "Come, sister spirit, come away!"

147. That singeth of the Indian wave,[29]
     Where beauty dwelleth in her cave;
     Amid the coral rocks we see
     The fairest flower of Araby!

Of him [30] who roamed from home and peace,
Drained Pleasure's cup, and died for Greece ;
Caught Dante's and a Tasso's fire
And struck anew each poet's lyre !

148. All hail, great Mother! long shall last,
The fadeless memory of thy past!
Thou art a blesséd beacon, sent
· To lighten up earth's firmament!
Thy science and thy songs do lie
Like stars athwart the mental sky !
And he, who great and good would be,
Must drink the streams that flow from thee.

149. Loveth man Justice? he must draw
Its precepts from thy Common Law ;
Thy Language, like a river flows,
Where right and justice ever grows ;
And on its long, extended banks,
Are ever growing lofty ranks
Of graceful cedars,[31] giving aid
To all who dwell beneath their shade !

150. Upon its fruitful valleys there,
Doth grow the Tree of Knowledge fair ;
And he who pluckcth its ripe fruit,
Shall swell the brightest, fairest troop
That ever trod the shining way,
Amid the broad effulgent day
Of truth and fancy, and of faith,
That triumphs over life and death !

151. Down on its all-pervading course,
Shall the great soul of Wilberforce
Pervade all climes, all lands instill
With a divine and generous will;
Till every land and every sea,
Are the abodes of Liberty!
And every seed that love hath sown,
Shall grow and bless some humble Home!

PART IX.

152. Ah! what is Home?   Is name or place
A home for man's exalted race?
Doth crib or larder, house or land;
Apparel, or the golden sand;
Knowledge of nature or mankind;
Meanness or nobleness of mind;
Unmeasured, fortunate success; —
Do these a real Home express?

153. Tell us, ye winds, as floating on
Your everlasting course ye run,
Where found ye, in the ancient time,
That pleasant land, that genial clime,
Where heart with heart, in constant bliss,
Mingle together; and they miss
No sun ray, by the Father sent,
To lighten up their firmament!

154. Tell us, ye waters, as ye lave
All lands with your encircling wave,
What isle, or continent, or rock,
Near or remote, escaped the shock,
When heavenly harmonies were stilled
Upon the earth ; and it was filled
With hissing discords, first began,
When sin had marred the primal plan?

155. Thou central Orb, bright God of Day !
Round thee the sister planets play :
Which of the luminous, shining train,
Know not the curse of sin and pain ;
Know not the lurking serpent's den,
His poisonous tooth ? most fatal, when
His pleasing, gaudy coil is shown
Where else had bloomed a happy Home.

156. Home ! fragrant flower ! from thee the dove
Drinketh its daily draughts of love ;
In thy soft colors [32] there doth dwell
A soothing, peaceful, holy spell ;
And underneath thy verdant leaves
The evening zephyr gently weaves
The woof that bindeth human hearts
In golden threads, till life departs !

157. Close by thee, — 'twixt the burning rays
Of life's unceasing, withering blaze, —
A stately Tree [33] its limbs doth spread,
Above the weary pilgrim's head ;

And underneath, and all around,
The seeds of human hope are found;
And on its bending branches grows,
The fruit that healeth human woes:

158. Perennial Tree! thou fadest not,
When human works and passions rot;
When priest and layman, king and slave,
Fill up the ever-opening grave;
When massive piles, built deep and high, —
Which scorn the earth, and time defy, —
Are buried 'neath the years to come;
Thy top shall point the spirit Home!

159. Thou, sacred Tree, shalt ever live!
And life's transcendent guerdon give;
When friends forsake, or pass away,
The joyous winds, that round thee play,
Whisper to weary ones, "Hope on;
Behind the clouds a glorious sun
Is shining, with resplendent beams!
Seen in the blessèd prophets' dreams! —

160. "Seen only when the earth is dim —
Left far behind; and when the hymn
Of saint and seraph mingle there,
Far, far above this grosser air!
Falls sweetly on the raptured ear,
When love and sorrow bring us near
The Holy One; and when the soul
Is full of Him, who maketh whole!"

161. Supernal Faith ! what would man be,
  If left alone of heaven and thee ?
  Of heaven and thee ? to thee is given,
  O Faith ! the golden gate of heaven !
  And through the crystal bars we see
  The visions of eternity !
  Dim, distant visions ! ye are worth
  More than the diadems of earth ! —

162. More than the flattering peans, sung
  By servile bards, to Fortune's son ;
  For sweeter sounds come floating near
  The obedient, loving listener's ear ;
  More than the welcomes, long and loud,
  To dizzy heroes from the crowd ;
  Too oft, alas ! the prelude sad,
  That driveth human frailty mad ! —

163. More than the fondest words of love,
  Breathed gently in the sylvan grove ;
  For truest vows are but the breath
  Of changing life, and end in death.
  More than the all-expanding mind,
  That shines supreme among its kind ;
  For highest types of power and worth
  Are sad, lone beacons on the earth.

164. Eternal God ! we bow to Thee
  The contrite heart and bended knee ;
  Great Fountain, whence all blessings flow
  To angels, and to men below ;

Whence cometh the seraphic fire,
That man and angel doth inspire :
Make earth in ages yet to come
To every soul a Happy Home !

165. Then faith, and hope, and every grace,
Shall dwell among our blessèd race ;
Then envy, hate, and war shall cease,
And then again the song of peace
Shall echo over hill and plain,
And angels dwell with men again ;
Then heaven to earth shall fondly come,
And earth shall be a Heavenly Home !

PART X.

166. HOME, Home in Heaven ! I fain would sing
Its raptures !   In the budding spring,
When the young, tender blade peeps forth,
So green, upon the smiling earth ;
And the pure snow-drop lifts its head,
Tenderly, on its virgin bed ;
When apple blooms perfume the air,
And warbling birds with joy repair
To verdant shades and trickling spring,
Their joyous notes of love to sing ; —

167. When fleecy flocks climb round the hill,
And feed 'mid pastures, calm and still ;
And when the sweet wild rose we seek,
With blushes on its lovely cheek ;
When blue flowers hang their clustering bells,
And cowslips clothe the fertile dells ;
When primrose blossoms, spreading far,
On every bank, each flower a star ; —

168. When the young feet with rapture stray
O'er hill and vale, each happy day ;
When age looks back with joy serene,
Adown the paths of living green ;
When poets dip the joyous pen
In dewdrops, each a precious gem ;
When rainbows span the deep blue sky,
To glad the heart and charm the eye ; —

169. When the maternal eye shines bright
Upon the infant's budding light,
And children sing the simple lays
That charmed us in the youthful days ; —
This, this is Home ! but not like heaven,
For mildew blights the buds at even.

170. Sweet Summer ! canst thou help me sing
Of Home in Heaven ? thy zephyrs bring,
'Mid orange groves and woodland song,
And lowing herds, a happy throng ;
'Mid golden sheaves and new-mown hay,
In the long, fragrant, joyous day ;

When the young fledgling learns to sing,
And ventures on his tender wing
To soar above the parent nest,
And glad returns at eve to rest.

171. Bring to the valley, full and round
At eventide, the curfew's sound ;
And kiss the milkmaid, blithe and hale,
Returning with her snowy pail !
Ripple the sparkling brooklet's breast,
Where finny denizens are drest
In gorgeous robes of sunny rays,
Basking beneath the noontide blaze.

172. The cooing dove, with joy elate,
Is murmuring love to listening mate ;
Float zephyrs o'er the flowers, and fill
With fragrance every vale and hill ;
And whisper in the bee's soft tone,
To the tired swain the song of home ;
But scattered wild-rose flowers lie riven,
And softly sigh, " This is not heaven ! "

173. O ! Autumn winds ! I list your lay
Of thankful hearts at opening day !
Thy ripening fruits in clusters crown
The trees, and bear their branches down,
Like honored age, with fruits all ripe,
Dropping to earth in gems of light ! —

174. Sing, gentle Autumn! sing to me
Of love, with all its ecstasy!
Of welcome home! from lips of love!
It lifts our tired hearts above
The toils of earth, and points to heaven,
Where changeless, endless love is given!

175. O! let your brown and yellow leaves,
Trembling and loosening in the breeze,
Breathe to my heart, how short the day
Of life; while loved ones seem to say,
"Cling not to earth, but come away!

176. "Yes, joyous come, if thou hast shed
Gladness and joy on hearts that bled;
If thou hast lifted up thy voice,
To make the weary slave rejoice;
If thou hast fed the poor with bread,
And soothed the sick man's weary head;
If thou hast cast a pitying eye
On wayworn travelers, passing by;
If thou hast wiped the widow's tear,
And left a silent influence there
Of joyous hope; — her upward gaze
Shall bless thee, more than loudest praise;
And He who loveth her shall wait
To ope for thee heaven's pearly gate!

177. "And if thy charity shall bring
The food that makes the orphan sing,

And prattling babes shall lisp thy name
In gladness, let the scroll of fame
Be silent ; for the angel throng
Shall sing for thee the conqueror's song!"

178. O! Autumn leaves! your colors blend
In hues and shadings without end!
Dear Autumn, let your sunbeams lie
In glory on the evening sky,
Till earth becomes a gorgeous dream,
And inspiration, like a stream,
Flows through the human soul ; till man
Is wrapped in Nature's wondrous plan!
And 'neath the burning, glowing dome,
His spirit sighs for Heaven and Home!

179. Fair Summer-Land! thy visions bring,
And teach these mortal tongues to sing!
Present to our astonished view
Translucent lakes, 'mid ether blue ;
And wafted barques, their waves to press,
And in those barques, — like flowerets drest
In love and beauty, — maidens bright,
Chanting sweet love songs, where no night,
With somber shades, and sickly dew,
Buries the loved ones from their view!—

180. Where Spring and Summer interblend ;
Where buds and blossoms fragrance lend
To every passing zephyr's sigh ;
Where, on the banks, the dear ones lie

Waiting, to give the welcome kiss ;
And sing the song of angel bliss ! —

181. Where Autumn's luscious fruits, all ripe,
'Mid clustering blossoms, bless the sight ;
And blushing fruits, and fragrant flowers,
Hang bending on the Eden bowers ;
Where smile forever loving eyes,
Those precious gems of Paradise !
Those stars, that leave our sorrowing sight,
To hide themselves in heaven's own light ! —

182. Where groups of fond ones wait to hear
The new-born footsteps drawing near,
Bringing the news of sorrow fled,
From the poor aching heart and head ;
Where sits the young-eyed Cherubim,
Chanting the child-like spirit hymn ;
And listening to the muse of fire,
Enchanting, sweeps Apollo's lyre
With rosy fingers, blithe and free,
In strains of moving melody ! —

183. Where sits the sire, of ancient time,
Endowed with wisdom most sublime ;
Smiling upon the happy throng,
And listening to each joyous song,
Till silence reigns ; then, calm and bland,
With parted lips and outstretched hand,
He points adown the fields of space,
Discoursing on the onward race

6

Of endless life ; its ceaseless march, —
Beneath the glittering, royal arch,
Studded with countless worlds afar,
Each world a happy, peopled star ! —

184. Relating wondrous tales of old ;
Each sentence grandly doth unfold
Truths written on the page of gold !
Truth knows no time ; it hath no space ;
Like God, confined within no place ;
'Tis ever old, and ever young ;
The choiring stars have ever sung
Its praise ; and space hath echoed back
The song, adown its endless track !

185. " Seek not (he said), O, infant man,
To antedate the primal plan ;
Ten thousand of earth's years I've scanned
Great truths ; and still on Ocean's strand
I wander ; and amid its sparkling sand,
Jewels of shining truth, more grand,
Lie undiscovered ; and I see
Labor for all eternity !

186. " Then onward, upward, be our cry !
While spirits through boundless ether fly,
Truth, still beyond, a radiant star,
Lights up the soul, and dwells afar ! "

187. He ceased ; — and than electric light
More quick, the vision left my sight !

And I, in mortal form below,
Stood silent ; for I could not know
Where they had fled ; I could not trace
The beauties of their dwelling-place !

188. I cannot sing the song I heard ;
Earth hath no pluméd, warbling bird
To sing that song ; and I must wait,
Till swingeth back the golden gate !
Then shall to us again be given
The hope of all, that real vision, —
Love's fadeless boon, — A HOME IN HEAVEN !

EXPLANATORY NOTES TO "HOME."

[1] Rape of Lucrece. — Shakespeare.
[2] Rainbow.
[3] Indian oratory.
[4] Small pox: first introduced by whites.
[5] On mid Mississippi are vast natural columns for many miles, resembling the ruins of ancient cities.
[6] Maize, or Indian corn, in immense fields.
[7] Vicksburg heights, the boasted western impregnable barrier of the rebels, was reduced July 4, 1863, as was also gained over them the victory of Gettysburg, by Meade over Lee, the day before, — giving us a double celebration of the Fourth of July.
[8] The cotton flower.
[9] This river lies between Virginia and Kentucky, slave states, on one side, and Pennsylvania, Ohio, Indiana, and Illinois, free states, on the other; extending over one thousand miles.
[10] Ohio River has vast coal mines on its banks.
[11] The entire population of Europe could be placed on the borders, or banks, of the Ohio, in a good position for independence, and within a few miles of its waters.
[12] The Ohio, and particularly the upper Mississippi, and mid Missouri and Kansas Rivers, have very fine, dark crimson sunsets bathing the entire horizon in all directions.
[13] Extensive works distill salt from springs, in large quantities, on the banks of the Ohio, in various places.
[14] The ten thousand Greek troops, under Xenophon, when returned from the Persian expedition, for young Cyrus.
[15] Napoleon.
[16] David and Goliah.
[17] Jesus to John, and his own mother.

84

[18] Caius Marcius was killed by the Volscians, through the jealousy of Aufidius, their native general, after he had defeated his own people for them.

[19] Sir Walter Scott.

[20] The hatred of English power, and of the Protestant religion, seems to be a complete barrier to the individual improvement and national resuscitation of the Irish people and nation.

[21] Will not this proprietary monopoly compel an exodus, like that of Ireland? and does it not now begin to cramp the enterprise and welfare of the English people?

[22] Are not the North Pole expeditions experimental insanities?

[23] Napoleon.

[24] 1620, December 14, Plymouth colony planted.

[25] The Great Trees of Yosemite, the " Siamese Twins," two from one root, one hundred and fourteen feet each in circumference; one, measuring one hundred and six feet in circumference, was two hundred and seventy-six feet in height. Some are three hundred and twenty-five feet high. The waterfall of the River Yosemite is twenty-six hundred feet, or nine times the height of Niagara, and the highest known.

[20] Milton. .

[27] Bunyan.

[28] Pope. `

[29] Moore.

[30] Byron.

[31] Men of Science, the Arts, Religion, Law, and Poetry.

[32] Home.

[33] Faith.

FEMME HEROIC.

I SING a Maid of lovely form,
Who 'mid the burr-oak trees was born,
Beside a stream of Indian name,
Where oft the Indian maidens came.
Her sire, from lands beyond the sea,
Sought the abode of Liberty,
And, on Atlantic's western main,
Rejoiced in Freedom's pleasing strain;
And while he sung, a western Maid,
Beneath the oak tree's cooling shade,
Gave back an echo through the grove,
And gentle zephyrs whispered love : —
Both listened to the zephyrs' breath,
And sang the love song until death !

The Maid I sing was first to greet
Their wedded love with infant feet ;
Hers was the first sweet infant smile
The happy mother to beguile ;
Her infant tongue the first to pour
Its prattling music o'er and o'er ;
Her rosebud lips the first to press
The mother's, in her fond caress ;
Her infant head the first to rest
Upon the mother's loving breast ;
Her tender hands the first to cling
Around life's orbéd, luscious spring ;
Her childish voice the first to play
Its bird-tones on the opening day !

And when this maid could trip along,
On tiny feet, and sing her song
Of infant joy ; when she could hear,
With sweet delight, the wild birds near ;
When to her soul the flowers could speak,
And in the morn her tender feet
Could wander down the distant meads,
Where cusha and the lambkin feeds ;
When the young mind's first opening light
Sees beauty in the dew-drop bright ;
When all the outside world appears
One glory, in the opening years ; —

Then the fond Trio went to dwell
Where the wild prairie flings its spell
Of vernal beauty ; where the flowers
Bloom gorgeous in the summer hours ;
Where the tall grass bends 'neath the storm,
And glistens in the dewy morn : —
'Twas here her early footsteps trod
The garden of the loving God !

Happy life ! happy day !
Where all strife flies away
From each heart ; where the smile
Doth not part ; but doth while
Every pain from the breast,
Till they gain endless rest !
Envy not state or pride,
Ye whose lot they deride ;
Envy not gold or land, —
Know ye not life more grand
Dwells with love, where they sing
Songs more sweet than notes of spring ?

How sweet the home of love ! here life begins
To the young soul on the dove's purple wings ;
Here, in the downy nest, the twittering brood
Are fed with love's divine, unceasing food !
Here in each voice love's music notes are heard,
And kindness tones the echo of each word !

Here the soft eye beams forth the happy smile,
And drives away earth's sadness and turmoil ;
Here chaste instruction lifts the heart to heaven,
And dear affection's changeless ties are given !

——◦◦◦——

This was the home of her I sing ;
Here did her dancing footsteps bring
The yellow-cup, and lily fair ;
The growing maize, with flowing hair ;
The bending sumach's crimson flower,
That decks wild Nature's verdant bower ;
The fleur-de-lis, with trenchant blade,
That blossoms in the distant glade ;
The bulrush, bordering on the lake,
And the cool, feather-netted brake ;
And that dear flower, that floats all day
Upon the lakelet's crystal spray —
That drinks all night the moon's soft beams,
And on its soft bed lies and dreams ;
That anchors in the oozy deep,
Where Nature's germs in silence sleep ;
That gambols when the south wind brings
The boisterous waves, and laughs and sings !
More fair upon the watery plain,
Than she of more pretentious name,
Who sailed upon the Cydnus wave,
And sleeps in her Egyptian grave.

She reigns supreme upon her throne,
And looks up to the great Unknown,
And bows her head to Him alone !
She asks not if the wide parterre
Of earth has flowers as pure or fair ;
She envies not their colors bright,
That drink the sun's unclouded light,
But blooms a modest watery star,
And mirrors back each world afar !
This flower spoke volumes to her soul
Of Nature's sweet, divine control ;
This water lily, like her heart,
Dwelt from the grosser world apart ;
And in its own sweet fragrance grew
Her spirit, nurtured by the dew
Of home affections ; — Virtue's nest ; —
The cradle where the love flowers rest !

Within the prairie cottage, kept with care,
Were youth's instructive volumes ; and her prayer
Was wafted on the evening winds to Him
Who lights the distant lamps, and dwells within
The deep profound, for truth, and inner light,
To read His never-changing laws aright.
She read the name of every leaf and flower,
And sung her father's songs within the bower
His hands had planted ; where was heard
The sweet voice of the unconfined wild bird,

That listened to the music of her song,
And lingered there, the purple grapes among !
And she was beautiful, where beauty reigned !
Not as the artificial flowers are strained,
Not as the slaves of fashion flash and shine,
But Nature's own sweet beauty, all divine !
Her eye had drawn from heaven's serenest light,
Soft as the moon, and melting on the sight.
The wild rose tinged her cheek, and blushing there,
Hid 'neath the drooping locks of flowing hair.
Her graceful form, moved like the thought of love,
When angels waft it to the realms above !
Her presence, in youth's happy, rural scene,
Was Nature's unassuming, smiling Queen ;
Her voice was like the evening zephyr's breath,
Or angel voices in the hour of death !
'Twas like the mother's first sweet song of praise,
When the young stranger gazes on her face !

----♦----

Blow, O Winds ! howling winds !
Winter winds ! moaning winds !
Lowering clouds, threatening clouds,
Pour ye down, howl ye down
Sorrows thick, sorrows fast !
Blast the bowers ; crush the flowers ;
Sever hearts, loving hearts ;
Crush the hearts ; break the hearts !

Grim old Death, chilly death,
Hateful death ! Spare not, Death,
Spare them not ; hear them not ;
Pity not ; tarry not !
Mother's love ; Father's love ;
Daughter's love ; Infant love ;
Parting words, sobs and words ;
Feeble words, broken words —
Spare not, Death ; heed not, Death !
Toll the bell, count the bell ;
Hear the bell, toll the bell !
Mourners meet, whispering meet ;
Mourners sigh, bend and sigh ;
Falling tears, flowing tears ;
Bursting tears ; burning tears !
Lonely rooms, vacant rooms ;
Hollow rooms, silent rooms :
Sullen doors, closed up doors :
Windows blank, windows closed :
Bed of love, downy bed ;
Pillows soft, pillows white,
Empty now, cheerless now !
Fireside sad, cheerless fire :
Songs of love, words of love,
Gone away, passed away :
Vacant hearts, burning hearts ;
Waiting hearts, breaking hearts !

Ah ! life is sad when friendships die !
  Sad is the soul when fond hearts leave ;
O ! prize their love when they are nigh,
  And to them strongly, firmly cleave !
Just as the milk-white lily's flower
  Oped its full petals to the sun,
Death stalked within Love's fragrant bower,
  And left the lovely flower alone !
Hast seen the lamb, in fertile meads,
  Famished, and sad, and lonely stray ?
So the dear maid her life now leads,
  For the sweet dam has fled away !
Her father ceased his cheerful song ;
  Her woodland walks are lonely now ;
The weary nights are dark and long,
  And heart and head in sadness bow !
Hast seen the youthful mother lie
  In death's cold, pitiless embrace,
With dreamless sleep closing the eye,
  And marble silence on the lovely face ?
O, mother's love ! sweet mother's love !
  Who hath not felt its matchless worth ?
It bids the soul's best passions move,
  And sanctifies the toils of earth.
And when the fountain sends no more
  Its crystal, limpid, sparkling spray ;
When love's sweet stream shall cease to pour
  Its gentle music on our way ;
Then sorrow sits like Egypt's night,
  And hangs its heavy-laden pall

On all that once was fair and bright,
    And shadows on our pathway fall.
O, Maiden fair! so young and fair,
    To thee this bitter cup was given;
This was thy first sad pang of care;
    The first storm on thy soul was driven!
The downy pillow drank thy tears;
    The sun's first rays thy tears enshrine;
And in the fast succeeding years
    Those bitter tears were ever thine!
But life rolls on, and in its way
    The storm and sunshine interblend,
And Nature's charms forever play
    Like sun rays, till the final end.

There's a charm on the earth, there's a charm in
    the sky!
There's a song in the soul, and a light in the eye!
There's a sunshine of hope in the morning of life,
And a sweet bow of promise that lightens the strife!
There's a confidence lives in the heart that is young,
And a halo of light on its pathway is flung!
There's a sound that we love in the youthful one's
    voice,
And the love that they bring makes the weary re-
    joice!
There's a beautiful world in the depths of the soul!
In the spring-time of life the sweet harmonies roll!

Then the garden of life has its roses in bloom,
And the visions we see have a joy and a plume !
'Tis a world of its own that the spirit moves in,
Ere the outer world brings its confusion and din ;
O ! the garden of life, with its perfume and flow-
 ers,
When the young heart reclines in Home's beautiful
 bowers !   .
There are clouds, there are storms, but the sun ray
 falls through,
And its silvery sheen sparkles bright in the dew !

Now, in her cradle's hallowed spot,
Where once had stood the natal cot,
Our blushing Maid, with tripping feet,
Ascends where men of wisdom meet ;
Drinks the clear stream that Science pours,
And enters in at Learning's doors.
Ere chanticleer, with clarion notes,
Proclaims the dawn ; ere Phœbus opes
The gates of heaven, what time the gray
Clouds usher in the morning ray ;
Before the milkmaid sings her lay
To listening herds, at opening day ;
While yet the clover drinks the dew,
Before the eye of heaven peeps through, —
Our early Maid hath left the nest
Where innocence and beauty rest ;

Where angels, all night long, did tread,
With silent footsteps, round her bed !
With loving heart and curious eye
She views the lambkins sleeping nigh ;
And at her silvery voice they rise,
Like innocence, in sweet surprise !
Where sorrow had the sad heart wrung,
And age the snowy locks had flung ;
Her quiet footsteps lingered near,
To soothe the sigh and dry the tear ;
And on the family table spread
The dainty meal, with home-made bread ;
Such as her mother spread before
The spoiler entered in the door ;
And on her brother's youthful brow
Impressed the kiss that lingers now !
Then, where the wise instruction give,
And for the young a garment weave
Of priceless worth ; where precepts flow
Like raindrops on the earth below, —
She stood amid the sages there,
A modest flower, so bright, so fair ;
So calm and still ; so good and wise ;
So deep and dark those melting eyes ! —
So steadfast, on the mental prize ! —
Like evening's star, when daylight dies !

. . . .

The prize was won ! the parchment scroll
Was like the sunlight to her soul !

7

Like Aaron's rod, with blossoms fair,
Or voices singing in the air !
Like golden dust to miser's eye,
Or angel voices when we die !

———◦◦———

'Tis the life of a God ! when the sower goes forth,
Scattering seeds that shall grow on the bosom of earth;
And the Maid that I sing went forth happy and free,
Sowing seeds that shall grow in the good time to be !
And the smile of her love made the sweet flowers
      grow
To the sunlight of heaven, from the dull earth
      below ;
The children clung round her, like lambs in the fold ;
And the precepts she gave were more precious
      than gold !
While the obdurate heart, that was heedless before,
Won by kindness and love, conned the lessons all
      o'er.
The fountain of life seemed to flow through her lips,
Like the nectar of flowers that the honey-bee sips !
And the sound of her voice was like music in
      spring,
When the breath of the south the first warbler doth
      bring !
Like the sound of the harp when the storm has
      passed by,
Or the welcome of love when the lover is nigh !

O, to see was to love her ! e'en age cast a sigh,
For the glance, ne'er forgot, from his first love's
sweet eye !
And the youthful heart leaped with a pleasure like
pain,
While the lovers laid siege to her heart, but in
vain ;
'Twas the world that she loved, like her garden of
flowers,
Which she pruned, and she propped, through the
summer's long hours,
And they gave back her love, as the echoing hills,
When the song of the bird down the sweet valley
thrills !
'Tis the hope of the world ! 'tis the prophecy's
breath !
The green laurels we weave for posterity's wreath !
'Tis the Nation's best hope, and her glory to-day !
'Tis the sword that the tyrants shall flee with dis-
may !
And the Teacher that works for the good of the
race,
Shall receive the reward in a happier place !

In the morning's silent freshness,
    When the early dew lies deep,
On the grass that bends with lushness,
    Where the hushed up crickets creep ;

Where the clover blooms in beauty,
    And the meadow-lark lies still ;
Where the ancient bending yew tree
    Clothes the barren rocky hill ;
Where the stream meanders slowly
    'Mid the willows, bending low,
And the dwelling of the lowly,
    Nestles 'mid the flowers that blow ;
Where the sun, in glinted glory,
    Drops his spangled gold-rays through ;
And heaven's perfumed breath so holy,
    Mingles with the censered dew !
Where the bright cascade is foaming
    Through the tangled wild-wood glade ;
And the antelope is roaming,
    'Neath the deep, umbrageous shade.
Where the speckled trout lie dreaming,
    'Neath the pebbly brooklet's breast ;
Where the sun's first rays are streaming
    On the bluebird's downy nest ;
Where the ivy-burdened elm tree
    Swings his century-dated arms ;
And the woodland echoes greet thee,
    Filled with Nature's choral psalms ;
Where the mountain bathes his forehead
    In the rumbling thunder storm ;
Gazing on the lowland florid,
    Where is heard the cottage horn ; —
There our Maiden often wandered,
    Wrapped in Nature's endless round ;

And in silent stillness pondered
  On the harmony profound !
When the winds sweep down the mountain,
  Blasting all beneath their breath ;
When the heavens' exhaustless fountain,
  Buries all the plains beneath !
When the sun breaks through in gladness,
  Smiling on the world below ;
And the sky forgets its sadness
  In the sun's enlivening glow ; —
Then she joins the blending chorus
  With the songsters as they sing
With all Nature, round and o'er us,
  Joyous as the notes of Spring !
And her merry laugh resounded,
  Where the happy children meet ;
Where the verdant lawn is bounded
  By the roses, fair and sweet !
Thus our Maiden, in life's morning,
  Drank morn's inspiration in ;
Thus the soul, in life's sweet dawning,
  Did its priceless guerdon win !
Thus the spirit, at life's fountain,
  Trembled at the opening door,
Gazing up the distant mountain,
  In the great forevermore !
Thus, O, thus her heart grew mighty,
  In the ever-opening strife !
And the loving God smiled brightly
  In her heart and in her life !

The roses are sweet, but the roses must fade ;
And the violets bloom where the loved ones are laid ;
And fresh is the morning that breaks on our sight,
But the morning soon fades into evening and night ;
The lily blooms sweet by the rivulet's side,
But the petals soon fall on the down-flowing tide ;
And the leaflet bursts forth in the Spring's wooing
  breath ;
But it fades, and it falls, in the winter of death.
O ! 'tis rapture to love, when the young heart beats
  high !
But the flowers of our love all blossom to die !
And the Summer's warm breath, and perfume so
  sweet,
Are but heralds that sigh of the Winter storm's
  beat.
There is rapture in birth, when the young life is
  born !
But death only waits for the beautiful form ;
And the life that sings on in its usefulness here,
Hath a sorrowful strain, with a lingering tear !
There's a beauty in life when we labor and wait
For the fullness of time, and the fiat of fate ;
When the hour hath its work, and the day hath its
  round,
And each word that we breathe hath a silvery sound !
But the harsh notes of woe howl a wintery blast,
And the smile hath a sorrowful tear at the last.
O, the world needs her heroes, her children of light !
But they fall from her side, like the meteor's flight ;

In their glory and might, in their beautiful noon,
They fade in the silence of death and the tomb !
O, the flower that is fair, the flower that is sweet,
Hath a life that is tender, and fragile, and fleet !
But the poison oak grows where the fragrant flower
      sighs,
In the sun's burning rays, till it fades and it dies !

———◆———

She loved : not as the infant loves,
    That sleeps confiding on the mother's breast ;
Not like the birds within the groves,
    Who sing their songs, then go to rest ;
Not like the flower, that views the sun
    All day, and drinketh in his beams,
Until his ardent course is run,
    Then sinks to rest, in dewy dreams ;
Not as the warrior loves loud fame,
    And dares the maddening hour of fate,
That he may leave a hero's name,
    And rest his ashes with the great !
Not as the monarch loves the crown,
    That circles round his regal head,
To tremble when he lays it down,
    To sleep with his ancestral dead ;
Not as the planets float around
    The central orb, that gives them light,
Content to trace the deep profound,
    And sing their love songs in his sight !

Not as the princess, in her pride,
    Loves the bright dower her monarch brings ;
And stands exultant by his side,
    The scion of a race of kings !
Ah, no ! she loved the soul within,
    Regardless of the tinsel's glare ;
Nor listened to the giddy din
    That Fashion mingles in the air ;
She loved the soul that toiled and burned
    With the grand fire that genius gives,
That through life's labors well had earned
    The meed of praise that ever lives ;
She loved the spirit that could look
    With curious eye on Nature's laws,
And in the ever-opening book,
    With rapture sought the primal cause ;
She loved the heart that Time had set
    His burning seal of love upon ;
And when they first in silence met,
    The mutual pledge of love was won !
As upward, from the Eastern gate,
    The rising sun to noon ascends,
So did their souls together mate
    In mutual love, that never ends !
·The world was theirs, and in its life
    They interfused a sacred gem
That calmed its passions and its strife,
    And wore it as a diadem !
Yes, they were one, by law divine ;
    That law that rules beyond control ;

That law, dear friend, is yours and mine —
  The law of love within the soul!
O, it was bliss to feel the breath
  Of sacred love, forever near!
It was an ever-verdant wreath,
  Forever fresh, forever dear!
And like the fabled Eastern maid,
  The child of Araby the Blest,
Whose spirit dwelt within the shade
  Of Oran's waters, in its rest; —
That wanders in the coral groves,
  Where evermore the bulbul sings,
And mingles in the sinless loves
  Of Fairies, clothed with golden wings! —
They felt the perfumed air of love
  In every sense, in every vein;
And all around, beneath, above,
  They heard its sweet, harmonious strain!
Conjugial love! fairest and best
  Of all the gifts to men below!
Soft pillow, where the soul may rest,
  And all its best affections grow!
O, it was theirs this love to share,
  In all its highest forms of joy!
Its ever-blooming flowers to wear,
  And in its light their lives employ!
Yes, life was sweet, whate'er befell,
  In health or sickness, joy or pain;
In shade or sunshine, it was well;
  And every loss was love's own gain!

O, joyous life ! when Nature brings
   The pledge of love to loving hearts !
The dear young life, that smiles and sings
   The song of home, till life departs !
'Twas beautiful ! that love-bred flower ;
   And on its fair and lovely face
There dwelt sweet Nature's subtile dower,
   That marks a high and noble race,
Within the eye a liquid light
   Lie deep and still, like distant heaven !
As if the soul must take its flight
   To the fair realms where life is given !
O, it was sad when the first blast
   Blew on the rare and budding flower !
And when the chilling winds, at last,
   Brought on the sad and fatal hour,
The angels waited round the bed
   On which earth's fairest love-flower lay,
And wreathed a garland round its head,
   To wear where garlands ne'er decay !

Little rosebud drooping ; Opening rosebud dying ;
Trembling petals peeping, Out upon the sunlight ;
Creeping in their sepals, Shrinking from the frost
    king ;
Drooping in the home bower, Breathing out its
    sweetness !
Love bird, drooping, singing, Trembling, swooning,
    springing !

Nestling in its warm nest; Sinking to its long
    rest;
Opening out in wonder, Eyes that want to slumber :
Wings that want their fleetness, Dying in their
    sweetness :
Spirit struggling, flying, Little baby dying ;
Parents crying, sighing — " Baby dying, dying ! "

O ! the angels could not spare her
    From the flowery walks above !
And the cherubs could not spare her
    From their balmy home of love !
The young Mothers could not spare her
    From the heaven of infant life ;
The sweet Cupids could not spare her,
    Struggling in this earthly strife ;
Heaven's heralds could not spare her
    From the swift-winged, fleeting throng ;
And Heaven's songsters could not spare her
    From their never-ending song !
Kindred spirits could not spare her ;
    They had watched the painful bed,
Wept and prayed, and lingered near her,
    Wreathed a glory round her head !
Now they bear her up, and onward,
    In the sparkling, starry dome !
Now they urge her spirit forward
    To the fairer, higher home !

And sometimes she bears a message
  From the happy throng above,
Swiftly in her distant passage,
  Burning words of hope and love !
Singing, singing, to each spirit,
  Sweetest music, soft and low ! ·
Mamma's soul was first to hear it !
  Mamma was the first to go !

———◦◦◦———

Sing on, O angels ! strike each golden wire !
Cherub and seraph, sound anew each lyre !
Open the portals of your sacred grove,
And sing anew your burning notes of love !
She hears your strains, she listens to your lay ;
She drinks the glory of your opening day !
Listen, O angels ! for the Æolian strain
That ushers in your midst her stainless name !
Sing on your love songs ! for her gentle voice
Shall join the strain, and bid your hosts rejoice !
Sing on your love songs ! she hath sung before,
In feebler tones, that music, o'er and o'er !
Press round her, take in yours her lily hand,
And give her welcome to your fairest band !
Press on her brow your purest, sweetest kiss,
And drown each tear in endless streams of bliss !
Bring to her soul the burden she hath borne,
And bid her cease forevermore to mourn ;
Let it forever dwell close to her side,
And roam with her through regions fair and wide,

And she shall tell the story of her birth;
The sorrows of the waiting ones of earth —
Their silent tears; the painful sighs that rise,
From human hearts, to spirits in the skies!
O! marvel not, ye dwellers here below,
That the blest, sinless regions overflow
With love to man! our messengers ascend,
Unceasingly, the ladder without end; —
Rehearse anew the sorrows that we bear,
And tell them of the crown of thorns we wear!
Sometimes she comes — the burden of my song —
Bringing heaven's fairest, loveliest flower along!
And on her waiting, faithful parent's head,
The fadeless, verdant wreath of love is spread!
And to his ear the fondest words are given,
That made the home of earth the gate of heaven!

Yes, she had fled from earth away;
　'Tis seldom hearts like hers remain;
They, like the angels, only stray
　One moment here, then mount again!
Her work was finished ere the sun
　Had quite attained his burning height;
But, O! she thought it just begun
　The hour she vanished from our sight;
Yes, blessèd soul! thy work is yet
　Before thee, in a higher sphere;
And thy bright sun shall never set, —
　It only leaves us sorrowing here.

The perfume of thy loving breath
   Shall bathe the hearts that think of **thee,**
And in the hour of pain and death
   Shall whisper of the life to be!
O, rural Maid, sweet Nature's pearl!
   The lovely flower become a star!
Unto our weeping eyes unfurl,
   The waving flag that floats afar!
We trace thy footsteps in the sand,
   On which we tread the daily round;
And when upon the mount we stand,
   We view thee in the vast profound!
In the dear garden of our love,
   Each flower more precious has become,
E'er since the angels placed above
   The fairest lily in her home!
Roll on, O Time! Thou canst not dim
   The vision of the coming day!
Thou canst not drown the distant hymn,
   That calls our spirits far away!
Thou canst not take our loved ones now,
   And drag them down to silent death;
Immortal glory crowns each brow,
   And life is *not* a fleeting breath.
Why do we sigh for those who sing
   The everlasting nuptial song,
And dwell in never-ending spring,
   The smiling, fadeless flowers among?
Life weaves no more dark midnight's pall;
   No more she gropes among the dead;

But smiles and sings amid them all,
 And shows the vision o'er her spread!
Lives of the wise, lives of the good,
 Ye cannot die, or cease to be;
No! Nature's laws have ever stood,
 And goodness lives eternally!
Thus Beauty cannot pass away, —
 She only leaves the dying flower
In every sunny beam to play,
 And smile afresh in Love's own bower!
Sleep on, O Maiden! Flowers shall spring
 Out of the dust that clips your form;
And little birds shall wait and sing
 Your praises in the opening morn!
Sleep on, young Mother! Fleecy dams
 Shall crop the lawn above thy breast,
And whisper to their little lambs,
 " Here Love and Innocence do rest! "
Sing on, O Mother! By thy side
 A lovely form is ever near;
And death shall nevermore divide
 The flowers of love that blossomed here!

———◆———

Farewell, farewell to Columbia's daughter!
 The fairest and best in the land of the free!
They were lonely above, 'till the death-angel
 brought her
To dwell with them there, by the crystalline sea!

Farewell tó thy form! 'Neath thé wide-spreading
  .prairie
It sleeps undisturbed in the Winter's cold blast;
Thy labors below for the heavens did prepare thee;
  And now thou art home, with the angels, at last!

The wild flowers bloom o'er thee, and give us a token
  That beauty but sleeps in its silent retreat;
And the pledges of love shall never be broken,
  But blossom afresh when the faithful ones meet!

The beautiful bow of the Day-king bent round thee,
  And doubled its colors to garnish thy rest;
It was silent and sad, when in death-sleep it found
  thee,
  And thought how it kissed thee in childhood's
  sweet nest!

We laid thee to rest, with our hearts full of sorrow,
  And buried the harp of our joy in thy tomb;
And the tears that we shed dimmed each beautiful
  morrow,
  And buried our souls in death's darkness and
  gloom.

Farewell to thy voice! 'Twas like music in sadness,
  When sorrow is lost in a beautiful song!
'Twas like chiming of bells in the hour of our glad-
  ness,
  And sings on our journey forever along!

But, O ! the dear heart, in its outgushing kindness !
It lives with us yet in the journey we go ;
'Twas the sunlight of heaven to the soul in its
blindness,
And dried up all tears in their sorrowful flow !

Farewell ! we will mourn thee while Sorrow's sweet
fountain
Shall flow from the hearts that are true in their
love ;
Till we leave the dull earth, to ascend to that mountain,
Where love-songs shall blend with the music
above !

Farewell ! till we meet where the heart sings for-
ever
The love-song it learned in the valley of tears ;
Where sorrow and parting shall come to it never,
And Love's highest hope to the spirit appears !

Farewell ! till we rove in the beautiful gardens,
Where fragrance floats on in the infinite time ;
Where the buds that we gave to the heavenly war-
dens
Shall blossom and grow in the ether divine !

Farewell ! till we gaze on the gardens of God,
That shall gladden our sight, like an infinite sea,
'Neath the glory that bends like a luminous flood,
O'er the beautiful Now, and the good time to be !

8

Farewell to the form that was earthly and mortal !
  Still thy spirit comes down to the loved ones of
      earth,
And lingers below, till we enter life's portal,
  To welcome us there to the spirit's sweet birth !

" Farewell ! " echoes back from the realms of the
      blest ;
  And it sings to our souls like the perfume of
      flowers !
And the love angels sing, — " It was best, it was
      best,
  For your loved one to come to our evergreen
      bowers ! "

MISCELLANEOUS POEMS.

LITTLE BELL.

WHO trippeth early down the dell,
Culling the white flowers and the blue,
Still drinking in the morning dew?
                    'Tis Little Bell.

Who greet I, in that happy spell,
When silence reigneth all around,
Where the soft greensward clothes the ground?
                    'Tis Little Bell.

Who, peering in the eastern sky,
Eagerly watch the sun's first beams,
As beautiful as angels' dreams?
                    'Tis Bell and I.

Who doth her joyous raptures tell,
Intoxicating my glad heart
With tones that never shall depart?
                    'Tis Little Bell!

Who, as the first bright sunbeams fell
On the swift running brooklet's breast,
Whispered me, of a land of rest ?
                    'Twas Little Bell.

Who kissed the cheek beneath her eye,
And said, " Together shall we be,
When we that land of rest shall see ? "
                    'Twas Happy I !

Why love I only thee so well ?
Because thy heart is ever bright,
And clothes thee in a happy light,
                    My Only Bell !

I bought thee, but I would not sell
The treasure that my love hath bought ;
Its richness, miser knoweth not, —
                    The Love of Bell.

Who saw the wild birds sing, and fly
Securely 'mong the forest trees,
Our hearts as light as was the breeze ?
                    'Twas Bell and I.

Who sent up holy thoughts on high
When gentle moonbeams played around,
And love its sweetest moments found ?
                    'Twas Bell and I.

Who marked the curfew's distant swell,
Whispering its music, O how sweet!
When we, my love, together meet?
     Thou, Loving Bell!

Who clingeth, when I say "Farewell,"
And presseth closer to my heart,
And softly saith, "We must not part?"
     'Tis Little Bell.

Who pledge the love that shall not die,
While the long years shall pass us by,
And say "Good night!" with many a sigh?
     Sweet Bell and I.

TWENTY-ONE.

I'M strong and free, and Twenty-one;
Joyous as a bird in the sun!
As full of hope, as full of glee,
As any son of man can be!
     I'm Twenty-one.

I care not for the childish days
I spent, when listening to the lays,
Sung by the cradle or the bed,
When soothing words or prayers were said:
     I'm Twenty-one.

I love to roam among the hills ;
The mountain breeze my spirit fills
With bounding rapture ! and I leap,
With springing joy, from peak to peak !
>> I'm Twenty-one.

I'd like a pair of wings, to fly
With the young eagles, up on high ;
I feel almost as light as they,
While watching their aerial play —
>> I'm Twenty-one.

I do not know, but sometimes think
They are a strange, mysterious link,
Uniting to a higher sphere
The human spirits lingering here.
>> I'm Twenty-one.

They seem to bear 'me in their flight
(As on and upward, in the light,
They vanish from my straining sight),
To regions where there is no night !
>> I'm Twenty-one.

'Twould be so good, while young and strong,
To soar up to the happy throng,
Like him who left the plains of earth,
Alive, to join angelic mirth !
>> I'm Twenty-one.

Departed fond ones ! I would come
And greet ye, now I'm Twenty-one !
But yet it would be hard to go,
And leave the loved ones here below.

     I'm Twenty-one.

And there is one I could not leave
Alone in sadness, here to grieve ;
Her spirit sings, with joy elate,
Because I am to be her mate !

     I'm Twenty-one.

Strange conflicts and emotions swell,
While memory flings her tender spell
Athwart my overflowing heart,
Like a magician's changing art.

     I'm Twenty-one.

Young life's a precious boon, I ween,
When love's sweet, tender light is seen
Smiling and bright ! for sadness flies
When love is seen in beauty's eyes !

     I'm Twenty-one.

And so I'm willing here to wait
My change, if it be soon or late ;
Hoping each coming day shall be,
As the glad time to-day I see,

     Now I am Twenty-one !

A BIRD.

I'm a meek little bird ; I fly and I sing,
And flutter aloft on my pluméd wing ;
I soar up above the grand lofty tower,
And twitter away each bright sunny hour !

I hide in the boughs of the leafy tree,
And sing out a clear, sweet melody
To my listening mate, in her downy nest,
Who shelters our young with her yielding breast.

I wander afar by the brooklet's side ;
On its pebbly, shining banks I provide
For our tender brood, and the watcher there ;
And swift to the nest of our love I repair !

I teach them to fly when the spreading wings grow,
And play 'mid the clover and daisies below ;
I sing to them softly, when back to their nest,
A sweet, dulcet lullaby, soothing to rest.

I live on in peace in the home that I love,
And I sleep in the boughs of the sheltering grove ;
Wake up with the sun, when he smiles in the east,
And chant to his praise, like a worshiping priest !

I borrow no sorrow, but sing while I may !
Sleep soundly all night, and live cheerful all day !
Confide in the care of the All-seeing Eye,
Through my short happy life ; and then — silently die !

THE GRASS.

LITHE, waving grass
Beneath our feet, bending so low,
Looking like limpid waves that flow
When the light zephyrs gently blow ;
  Thus passions pass.

The floating winds
Play on the grass, and heedless sing
Upon the honeyed insect's wing ;
And on th'Æolian sylvan string,
  Bring carolings.

Velvety lawn !
Soft as maternal, loving breast,
Where childhood found its sweetest rest,
And lost its fears when fondly prest,
  At eve and dawn.

Ah ! modest grass ;
Could we but dwell in the same place,
'Neath the sweet heaven's bright smiling face,
Like thee, and cease Ambition's race,
  'Twere well, alas !

Alas ! alas !
We, like the winds, pass heedless on,
Kissing each flower, till one by one
They wither, and our hopes are gone,
  Like faded grass.

O, faded grass !
We sometimes hope, like thee, to live
In gentle beauty, and to give
A deathless influence, that shall weave,
  Before we pass •

  Beneath the sod,
A fadeless garment for the soul,
Make many a sorrowing spirit whole
On earth, and point a better goal
  Above, with God !

  Then, when we fade,
The winds shall spread the fragrant smell,
And sing the loving, last farewell;
And many a lowly fond one tell
  Where we are laid.

  And we shall rise,
When the kind Father looks around
For sleeping children in the ground,
And with his favored ones be found
  Beyond the skies !

THE COURIER.

HAD I to choose a name, a blesséd name,
To place upon the scroll of present fame,
Or grace the annals of the coming age,
Whose light shall fill a brighter, better page ;
I'd not be called a King, with sparkling crown,
Before whose presence, and whose august frown
Encircling courtiers feared, and smiled, and bowed ;
Whose ear was ravished by the thoughtless crowd ; —

I would not be a plodding slave to wealth,
And, to be called a rich man, give up health,
And loving friends,_and happy, happy home,
And sweet reflections in the time to come !
I would not crave the name of him who leads
The minds of men with honeyed words, and pleads
The cause of passing passion to the ear,
That prompts the worthless, senseless, transient
   cheer
Of lust and hate ; for these shall pass away
Like Chaos, in the light of coming day !

But, O ! I'd drink the streams of wisdom past,
And learn from errors in the ocean cast
Of Time's deep surge, the lessons that shall live
Forever in the spirits that survive
Their transient reign ; would show the lessons bright
To earth's increasing multitudes, with light

Drawn from the colors Nature's cunning weaves,
In beauty, in her flowers and trembling leaves;

Drawn from her power, in watery torrents seen;
Her love, in every radiant, sunny beam;
Her voice, that speaks upon the pelting blast;
And her sweet silence, in the valleys cast
On evening zephyrs.   Silence, O how sweet
To kindred spirits, who by moonlight meet
To whisper loving words to listening ears,
In youth's fresh joy, when future life appears
Like the fond vision, painted in the soul
Of purest saints; their heavenly, happy goal!

I'd be the Courier of the coming time,
To fill the thirsty soul with news divine;
The hasty messenger, with willing feet,
To lift the poor from the recumbent seat
Of hopeless, aimless life, and fix his eye
On noblest aims; which in his soul shall lie
Like precious jewels, sparkling like the dew;
And like the dew upon the thirsty flower,
Refreshing every laboring, weary hour:
I'd smile away the dark, receding night,
And like the Day-star, fill the world with light!

FRIENDSHIP.

HAST found it? — Hold it fast; ay, feed it
With nectar from the gods!
If life is young, thou knowest not its
Priceless worth : O, what odds
To thee, if Fortune's rods —

Pursue thee? If thy friend is by thee,
Then thou art still a host;
Thy strength shall give thee wings like eagles',
Quick to the peaceful coast
To bear thee; this thy boast —

Thou hast a friend! I've seen misfortune
Leaning on its staff: bright
Was the eye; though poverty, with rags,
Proclaimed its deadly blight,
Love lent her kindly light!

Gold cannot buy it; O, richer far
The poorest wretch with this,
Than the hard miser counting his hoards;
It giveth purest bliss,
And bringeth gentle peace.

Princes and kings have lived without it —
O, no! they have not lived!
(It is not every one that drinketh in

Earth's air hath truly breathed
The breath of life :) they've weaved —

A little web ; admired its colors ;
  Worn it as a robe ; glad
When the crowd admired it too ; listened
  For their applause ; grew sad
  When rage and scorn were mad.

Wouldst have a friend ? Seek virtue, goodness,
  In their gentlest dress ; pride
Formeth not the casket where it dwells ;
  Draw to thy loving side
  Tried ones, long to abide.

The restless Corsican, when lonely,
  Found one ; and such a one
Is found alone by Fortune's favored
  Sons ; ah ! the bright sun
  Forsook when she had gone !

He knew her worth when brooding on the rock ;
  And in his latest hour
He called in vain ; the broken heart was
  Still ; the sad, withered flower
  Was safe, beyond his power !

But He of Galilee, He found it !
  Amid the fiercest scorn
Of pride and passion, the lowly ones

Loved him since he was born,
Till the sharp crown was worn.

Then, dying, he bequeathed it, left it
With his little ones ; gave
It to the sons of light, the sons of God ;
And the pure soul shall have
Its full fruition far beyond the grave !

FAREWELL.

TIME flieth : we must part,
Perhaps forever ! Why,
Why do we shrink and start
When precious moments die ?
All things are thus on earth ;
The sweet, fond mother's kiss,
That clings to us from birth,
Alas ! too soon we miss !

The careless joy of youth
In the full prime is lost,
While its glad, gushing truth
On the world's wiles is tost :
And manhood's ardent hope
Expires in the full prime ;
And the sad heart doth grope
Before the parting time.

Why doth the spirit cling
  To Friendship's pleasant spell,
While every breeze doth bring
  Upon its wings — Farewell?
We are but bubbles, thrown
  Upon the howling blast,
Lost in its dying moan,
  In silent caverns cast!

We dream — but stubborn Fate
  Stands like the rocky height;
And while we fondly wait,
  The vision leaves our sight:
Poor dreamers — it is dark
  When we awake to see;
And the strained eyeballs smart
  In night's infinity!

One word, alone, is left
  To mortals lingering here;
And the dense cloud is cleft
  With its bright flashing spear!
O, it is Faith, that sings
  The distant, heavenly hymn;
And through life's winter brings
  The ever-budding spring!

O, may its music swell
  Through all life's coming days;

And softly whispering, tell,
  In sweet Æolian lays,
Of happy scenes in store
  In the dear land of light ;
Where friends shall part no more,
  And faith is lost in sight !

—◦•◦—

MOTIVE.

WHAT dost thou live for ?
Livest thou for the baubles of a day, —
For self-adornment ?   Doth the sparkling gem
Fill up thy fancy, and thy soul contemn
  The poor, courting the gay ?

What dost thou live for ?
Livest thou for these ?   The poor butterfly
Is wiser far than thee ! for he doth leave
His wings before the wintry winds bereave
  .   Him, and before he dies !

What dost thou live for ?
The antelope is freer far than thee !
He flies before the winter, and his breast
Inhales the mountain breeze, where he doth rest :
  Thou art not half so free !

9

What dost thou live for ?
Must Immortality preserve thy name
To distant generations ? ` What is this
To thy repose ?   Is there one drop of bliss
    Sealed in the urn of fame ?

What dost thou live for ?
Is it the bound that circumscribes thy lust,
That satisfies thy longing, human soul?
The crawling reptile comprehends the whole,
    Trailing in slimy dust !

What dost thou live for ?
Dost imitate the sponge, that sucketh up
The ocean, in his dark, voracious cell ?
Filleth thy barns and stores, and saith, — " 'Tis
    well " ?
    How pitiful thy lot !

What dost thou live for ?
Be a living soul !   Up to thy manhood !
Let the serpent drag his grovelling circles
On the slimy soil ; low passion dulls
    The higher, greater good.

What dost thou live for ?
Life is an ample field for noblest toil ;
Thou need'st not stoop below thy fittest place ;
Enough remains to do among thy race ;
    Thy soul thou need'st not soil.

What dost thou live for?
Live for the captives; make their spirits free;
Spare not thy life when human wrong stands by
Imploring help! Be strong: thou canst not die!
Thy Father keepeth thee!

What dost thou live for?
Fill thy heart with love: purest love to God
Will make thy spirit grow; and mighty deeds
From thy right hand, for human needs,
Shall break Oppression's rod!

What dost thou live for?
Is life made so short that thou shouldst trifle
With the golden moments? Work in earnest!
Expand thy powers! be sure thy firmest
Thoughts thou dost not stifle.

If thus thou livest, trouble not thy soul
With future ills; thou hast a better goal
In the invisible, eternal sphere,
Than all thy happiest thoughts have painted here:
And when thy life is " rounded with a sleep,"
Some human hearts for thee shall fondly weep
The tears of joy, and in the blessèd light
Of coming heaven a crown shall cheer thy sight!

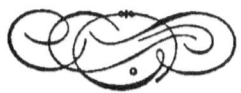

SHADOWS.

Past, past forever, vain struggles of youth;
Ah! past forever its faith and its truth;
Past, past forever its madness and mirth;
And past forever the glitter of earth:
   Shadows and shapes memory takes;
   Shadows that fly rapidly by;
   Shapes full of light, sinless and bright,
   Come in the night, blessing my sight!

Farewell to the hopes that lingered and sighed;
Farewell to the passions that lure and deride;
Farewell to the prospect that filleth the eye
With beautiful shapes, that blossom to die!
   Sweetly and low, floating below,
   Under the trees, on the light breeze,
   On my quick ear, cometh so dear
   (Sent from above), music of love!

Time mocketh while the bauble slips;
Time painteth red the dewy lips;
Time laugheth when the eye is bright,
But grinneth when it dims the sight:
   Ah! cruel Time! the sport is thine;
   Thy jeers and gaffs, thy merry laughs,
   Thy scoffing wit, doth ever sit,
   Mocking the brave, o'er waiting grave!

Adown the ages shadows flit
And dance where gods and monsters sit,
Move softly round each sculptured tomb,
And haunt the ruined banquet-room :
  Crumbling slowly shrines once holy ;
  Shades grow shorter round each altar ;
  Letting sunlight, as a birthright,
  Spread, and cover earth all over !

Farewell to the shadows and shapes of the past !
Farewell to the groans that swelled on the blast !
Hail, songs of the mountains, that sing of the free,
And blend with the base of the limitless sea !

CUPID.

Vexing, little, dimpled boy ;
Come, and fill me full of joy !
Wounded, at thy feet I lie,
Since thou had'st thy arrows fly,
Rankling, like a poisoned dart,
In my inmost, panting heart,
Subject to thy cunning wiles,
Chilling flights, and winning smiles ;
Sleepless nights, and languid days,
Follow thy fantastic plays.

Often, as I look around,
Listening for the gentle sound
Of thy pinions in the air, —
Looking for the form so fair, —
Sweetest music fans thy wings ;
Sweetest, that the zephyr sings !
'Neath the stars, it murmurs on,
When the busy day is gone ;
And the moon her softest light
Lendeth to thy song all night.

Daylight hath no charms for me ;
In its blaze I cannot see
The bright, lovely light that thou
Bringest on thy radiant brow !
Dreaming all day, while the sun
Moveth in his glory on,
I, 'mid all things else most dull ;
Emptiest, when all else is full.

Come, O come ! thy arts employ ;
Turn my sadness into joy ;
Take me in thy fond embrace ;
Plant sweet kisses on my face !
Then I will not let thee rove ;
Then I will hold fast my love,
Till I feel no more alone, —
Till we *are forever One !*

PEACE.

Sweet, gentle Peace! sweet as the air
Bathing the weary brow of care
In citron groves, and spicy bowers,
Under the moonbeam's silent hours.
Sweet is the hour when strife is mute;
When, listening to the lover's lute,
The silent fond one, rapt and still,
Drinketh of love the spirit's fill!

Sweet as the curfew's distant sound,
While the one precious form is found,
Waiting to hear the welcome voice,
Laden like gales from Paradise!
Whispering the vows forever dear
To the glad, listening, lover's ear!
Those vows that never leave the heart,
While dwelleth there the living spark.

Sweet as the memory of the past,
The look of love, the first, the last!
Sorrow and time take not away
The raptures that forever play
Like shining plumes on Memory's wings;
Long as the natal angel brings
The first bright light of other days
That lingers in his purest lays.

Gentle, O gentle as the sound
Of kindest words, where love is found ;
Like cooings of the gentle dove,
When zephyrs dally in the grove ;
O, heavenly guest ! forever dwell —
Forever let thy music swell
In this fair earth, that all may know
What blessings from the Father flow ; —

Blessings as ample as the air ;
Blessings that all his creatures share ;
For all around, above, below,
The germs of sweet fruition grow ;
Full, pregnant buds, striving to peep
From the green husks in which they sleep ;
Waiting the sunshine and the dew
To bring their beauties to our view !

O, holy Peace ! man cannot be
An angel till he loveth thee !
O, laboring Earth ! when shall thy breast
(Which gives to the departed rest)
Be found as soothing, soft, and mild
To thy sad, weary, living child ?
When shall old War and Discord cease,
And every heart be filled with peace ?

I hear its dulcet song of love
Warbled in every shady grove ;

And on the evening's globes of light,
It falls like sun-flakes, pure and bright;
It murmurs in the brooklet's glee,
And in the cascade's ecstasy
It leaps for joy ! and every breeze
Singeth in praise to thee — O Peace !

MY GARDEN.

WHEN Phœbus peepeth o'er the hills,
And winds blow fresh, my spirit fills
With bounding joy ; and on the ground
I fondly look, for there is found
       My Garden !

'Tis very large, and very sweet,
And many a flower the eye doth greet ;
'Tis interspersed with many a grot,
And many a sloping, grassy spot —
       My Garden.

I do not vex the earth, or sow,
Nor toil, nor sweat, to make it grow ;
Nor plodding proxy place I there,
To take beneath his pruning care
       My Garden.

I have no parchment title-deed,
Yet doubt I not my right : I read
It on the ancient record, left
To me and mine, an endless gift —
      My Garden.

I mean, 'twas given to him who bore
My name : wide as the ample floor
Of earth and ocean are its bounds !
And far as Nature's music sounds !
      My Garden.

Our family is very large ;
Yet none are pushed beyond the verge
Of the estate ; for even where
A brother dwells, I find just there
      My Garden.

Some sickly child looks rather sour,
When I intrude upon his bower ;
But when I point him to the sky,
He breathes to me in a soft sigh —
      " Thy Garden ! "

Some brethren toil, and labor hard
To fill some little spot, and guard
Its beauties from my loving gaze ;
Then the tall trees proclaim the place
      My Garden !

One curious flower is ever nigh
My loving heart, and fills my eye
With constant pleasure, for I see
Its fragrant blossoms bloom for me !
                    My Garden.

It maketh every other flower
More precious, by its gentle power ;
Clings to me fondly, while I gaze
On Nature's beauties, and I praise
                    My Garden.

O ! what were Nature without thee ?
Her beauties concentrate for me,
In the sweet depths, that in thy petals lie !
And most of all, I there espy
                    My Garden.

I do not think my eyes will weep,
If thou art with me when I sleep,
And wilt but promise me to dwell
Still there, where we have loved so well —
                    My Garden !

How many precious hours I've spent
Beneath the smiling firmament,
Gazing thy growing charms to see,
Dreaming of love, and heaven, and thee,
                    My Garden !

On every flower, shrub, vine, and tree,
Hangeth a precious memory !
And the soft greensward where I lie,
Transports me to the rest on high —
Our Garden !

PASTORAL.

Ye living lawns, and wide-spread meads !
Where Love her little lambkins leads ;
Where Peace, adown the flowery dell,
Weaves in the soul her quiet spell :
Where murm'ring waters gently flow,
And lowing herds at noontide go
To drink the cool, refreshing stream,
And in its music sweetly dream !
Where wild-birds chant in every tree
The matchless song of Liberty !
Where sweetest flowers, of various dye,
Smile on the Day-king passing by ;
And when he sinketh in the west,
They calmly take their evening rest,
To sleep all night, beneath the spheres,
And wake in Morning's dewy tears.

O, silent walks, to friendship dear !
When Evening's social hour draws near ;
And the soft summer zephyrs sigh
To Day's last beams, that fade and die ;

Where dwells the maiden, mild and fair,
'Mid Nature's scenes, and her sweet air ;
With heart as pure as mountain rills,
And joyous thoughts her bosom fills,
As in the groves she strolls and sings,
And drinks from Nature's sparkling springs ;
Culling the flowers with loving care,
To grace her flowing golden hair ;
Tripping along, with joyous feet,
Some loving swain with smiles to meet ;
With sinless heart and guileless eye
To Love's unsullied arms to fly !

How calm the Sabbath morning dawns
Upon the verdant, wavy lawns !
How tranquil is the Sabbath rest,
In Home's secluded cottage nest !
What cheerful songs the children sing,
Where craggy rocks their echoes ring !
Reverent and solemn, age and youth
Listen to words of love and truth ;
The lengthened locks, as white as snow,
Like threads of silver, wave and flow
From honored heads, that soon shall sleep
Beneath the dews that gently weep !
How solemn, when the form lies low,
And tears of fond affection flow
From kindred hearts and ancient friends,
When life its devious journey ends !

Then faults are buried in the dust,
And Faith looks up with fearless trust
To Him who gave the infant breath,
And called the spirit home in death !

Sweet Home ! amid the valleys green !
Thy loveliest light is ever seen
Where simple, honest hearts are found,
And mingled songs of joy abound ;
Where Passion's curse hath never trod,
And Nature sings a loving God !
Where kindness flows in every voice,
And makes the weary heart rejoice !
Where age is calm as summer air ;
And youth is blithe, and free from care ;
And in the bonds of love are bound
Age, youth, and childhood's happy round !

Hence, curséd Lust ! your seething pool
Is found in cities : every fool
Flounders and grubs within your sty ;
The sensual, bloated, bloodshot eye
Gloats on the shadow thou hast made,
And rots and festers in its shade.

God made the country, and its flowers !
Its sunny slopes, and shady bowers !
Its clustering shrubs, and giant trees,
That sing and murmur in the breeze !

Its warbling birds, and lowing kine ;
The mountain-top, and precious mine ;
Its wide-spread lake, and pebbly brook !
Each character in Nature's book
Stands out before our raptured sight,
An endless flood of living light !

YOU AND I.

Up and down, far and nigh,
All belongs to you and I ;
When the sun gilds the east,
He is mine, and I his priest :
When the clouds mount up, and fly
In the deep cerulean sky ;
When they cast beneath the sun
Shadows on the horizon ;
When they rise, so pure and white,
Filled with Heaven's unsullied light ;
Like fleecy hills, built of snow,
Where the sun's bright rivers flow ;
When they drop down on the land,
Drops as round as grains of sand ;
When they're clashing in the fray,
Where the vivid lightnings play !
When they're sleeping in the west,
Where the sun has gone to rest,

Glowing in their golden dreams,
Drinking in his gorgeous gleams !
When they're hanging like a pall,
Where the midnight vapors fall : —
Through all shades of changing time,
They are God's, and God is mine !

See yon tall and stately tree,
Waving where the winds are free ;
Where the eagle builds its nest,
That its callow brood may rest ;
Where the squirrel hides its young ;
Where the skylark pours his song ;
Where the wild flowers blush unseen,
In their beds of living green ;
And the fleet-foot antelope
Gambols down the grassy slope ;
Where the living, sparkling spring,
First begins his wandering ;
Where the dew-drops, clear and sweet,
In the wild-rose petals meet,
Sleeping there till Phœbus brings
Morning on his golden wings, —
— Painting with his magic brush
Nature's pink and pearly blush ;
Where the evening zephyr brings
Perfume on its downy wings —
Breathing in the floweret's breast
Gentle sleep and balmy rest :

Loving friend, these all are thine;
They are God's, and thou art mine!

Silent depths, unknown, divine,
Where the far-off sun-flakes shine;
Worlds unseen, and seen afar
In each distant tiny star:
Harmony sublime and grand,
From Creation's boundless strand,
Chimes forever through its maze,
To the all-Creator's praise!
And the ethereal wind-harps round,
Echo back the notes profound!

Beauty dwells above, below!
And its gentle wavelets flow
All around, where'er we go;
And its buds and blossoms grow
On the mountain, in the glen,
Decking Nature's diadem!
Dwells in the heart, in the eye,
And in the soul's deep melody!
In the scattered words of love;
In the meadow, and the grove;
On the earth, and in the air;
In the song, and in the prayer;
In the smile, and in the tear;
Always ours, and always near!
In the depths of human woe;
In the heaven to which we go:

.   Beauty's fount, unspent, sublime,
Is ours, dear friend, 'tis yours, and mine.

Oceans lave each distant shore,
Round and round forevermore ;
Calm and silent in their sleep,
As the infant's slumber sweet !
But when winds and storms arise,
Leap in fury to the skies !
Bearing on their dashing waves
Human hopes and human graves ;
Beating on the rock-bound coast,
In the furious tempest tost,
Precious freights and precious hearts,
While Hope's anchored cable parts,
Burying in the dreadful deep
Fond hearts, that shall forever sleep !

Weep not, though they lie so still ;
'Tis the good Creator's will :
Let our spirits look above
For the absent souls we love !
They no more are tempest-tost ;
They shall never more be lost ;
They have fled the briny wave,
And escaped the deep, dark grave :
They have fled, but they are free
As the wide, unfettered sea !
They have left our mortal sight,
Lost to us, but lost in light !

Like the sun that sinks to rest,
In the dying, fading west,
Soon again to rise and shine,
Full of love and light divine !
Love can never, never die !
Nor, dear friend, can you or I.

———◆———

OUR DAISY.

Sᴀᴅ the refrain, with silent tears,
  That flow like raindrops while we praise thee ;
And memories of departed years
  Sing round our souls, of gentle Daisy !

'Twas sunshine to the mother's heart,
  Fed by thy smiles to love and praise thee ;
And to our eyes the grave looks dark
  Where sleeps so sweet our gentle Daisy !

Sigh soft, O zephyrs, o'er her bed !
  O song-bird, sweetly sing, we pray thee !
Grow soft and green over her head,
  O verdant lawn, above our Daisy !

Wave lithe and graceful o'er her grave,
  When chilling fogs hang dark and hazy,
O weeping willow, true and brave !
  Over the sleeping form of Daisy !

Cluster, O wild flowers, o'er her head!
    Drink endless sunbeams, bright and mazy;
The form below is cold and dead;
    But sweetly blooms above our Daisy!

O, for the vision of the blest!
    In the sweet summer-land to trace thee,
Where thou art singing in thy rest,
    " Come, loved ones, come and dwell with Daisy!"

EXCELSIOR.

RISE up, O heart, my heart!   O, soar and sing!
    Though clouds ingulf thee, they shall pass away,
And Time shall bear thee on resistless wing
    Beyond these fogs, up to a brighter day!

No more Night's sombre pall hangs o'er the plains;
    No more the spirit gropes among the dead;
But Day's unsullied opening splendor reigns,
    And Life's full, radiant landscapes beauties spread!

No more shall Hate his impious brow adorn
    In regal splendor, torn from Virtue's breast;
But Love — sweet infant in the manger born —
    Sings to the soul her song of endless rest!

Blow on, impious Winds ! make oceans roar !
Lash fearfully the sailor's fragile shell !
He supplicates the deaf sea-god no more,
    But 'mid the storm sings calmly, " All is well ! "

No more the soul of fire sings his sad strain
    In hopeless tones of sorrow and despair ;
For after death he strikes the lyre again,
    And sings more sweetly in his native air !

Farewell, farewell ! the fond ones whisper low,
    While on the dying couch the dear one sleeps ;
But not farewell forever ; for they know
    Eternal Life her own dear children keeps.

O, what is life ?   Is transient, changing time,
    That circumscribes the heaven-born soul below,
Where harsh notes drown the heart's melodious
        chime — -
    O, is it here that life must live and grow ?

Ah, no ! we are but travellers passing through
    The lowlands, where the air is dank and drear ;
Where flowers scarce drink the clear, refreshing dew
    Before they fade, and leave us sorrowing here.

Then sing, O loving heart ! though sorrows press,
    And pierce thee with the sharp and barbéd spear ;
Behold, the earth puts on her cloudy dress
    Before her star-eyed, fragrant flowers appear.

The sun of life shines bright above them all ;
  Still brighter shines as up the mount we tread ;
And soon heaven's gorgeous sun-illumined wall
  Shall, like a glory, on our vision spread !

OLD HOME.

I come to thy breast, O, Native Home !
To drink of the limpid, sparkling foam
That I quaffed with zest in youthful days,
In the summer sun's bright burning rays.

I come to hear the sweet wild-birds sing,
As they used to do over the spring,
When my brothers filled the shining cup,
And laughed in my eyes while I drank it up.

I come to hear each familiar voice,
Which made my young, bounding heart rejoice ;
To hear the old songs that mingled there,
So wild and free, in my native air !

I come to rest my sad, weary head
On the soft old downy yielding bed :
It is fevered now, and needs repose
From the burning tears and silent woes.

Thy sparkling waters are leaping still;
But where are the feet that ran up the hill
So fleet and glad when my heart was light?
O, cruel Time! hast thou dimmed my sight?

I hear them still, the sweet birds so free!
But I do not hear the young, boyish glee,
Nor the floating tones of my sister's song,
Awakening echoes the hills among.

O, tired heart! Ah, why did it come
To sorrow, and break in the dear old Home?
It cometh but once, that youthful time;
But I love thee still, thou Old Home of mine!

MUSIC.

Mysterious power! unseen, but felt
By all; making the passions melt
In the shrill numbers that are heard
From the sweet spirit of each bird;
Or in the tones that float afar
On zephyrs' wings from some guitar,
That mingles with the lover's sigh,
Or fills some infant's lullaby.

'Tis heard in the pure mountain breeze,
Turning the branches of the trees

Into sweet harp-strings, while they sing
The burden of each happy spring!
Or with a bold, sharp, wintry hand,
Which forest monarchs scarce withstand,
Striking their gnarléd limbs apace,
To a grand, wild, sepulchral base!

'Tis heard in childhood's happy glee,
Where'er it roameth bright and free,
Where violets and bluebells bloom,
And Nature giveth ample room
For the young feet to bound and leap
Out where the speckled lizards creep;
Where happy frogs express their joy,
And angling arts the time employ. —

And how their swelling hearts rejoice
To hear the music of her voice
Who wearies not, but like the dove,
Sings her unchanging notes of love!
Unchanging while that dove remains;
Unchanging till the parting pains
Bring the sad period to the lays
That filled the home of youthful days.

Farewell, soft lays! Though ye are past,
Ye dwell as long as life shall last
In our sad hearts. O, there remain,
Till angels chant the dying strain!

Ay, even then those lays shall cheer
The longing, listening, loving ear,
That dying, grasps each precious sound
That mingles with the angels round !

Calm Evening ! music floats around
In thy enchanting curfew's sound ;
And echoed by surrounding hills,
Day's wandering, weary passions stills ;
Soothes the sad spirit with its power,
And bringeth back each happy hour
On Morning's swift and pluméd wings,
Which Evening in her stillness brings.

Ah, precious moments ! sad but sweet,
When gentle sounds of loving feet
Come tripping round in the soft breeze
That danceth through the quivering trees ;
And every leaf on which I tread
Sounds like the footsteps of the dead,
Come in the evering air to tell
The sadness of the last farewell :—

Come in the evening air, to know
If the same fragrant blossoms blow
In fadeless beauty here below,
Like those where blesséd spirits go !
They change not in the home above,
Where doubt nor fear shall cloud the love

Too pure for earth, to good to stay
Where all the lovely pass away !

Come, viol of the magic ring ;
And thou, soft flute, thy warblings bring ;
And thou, of more pretentious string,
Whose numbers charm us while we sing ;
And come, O sweet, harmonious reed,
Whose quivering tremulo doth plead,
In moving sounds, sweet Pity's tears,
While Sorrow's melting lays she hears.

But thou, whose moving, melting fires
Devotion's noblest strain inspires ;
Thou of the deep, tremendous bass,
Whose vast capacities embrace
All other sounds of pipe or string,
Blending with human tones, which sing
Enrapturing songs, — your music bring,
And make the aerial concave ring !

Music 's the medium to the skies,
By which, on holiest thoughts, we rise
Into His presence, ever blest,
Who giveth joy, and peace, and rest !
Without sweet music, man would be
Unfit, O God ! for heaven and Thee :
But filled with harmony and love,
He enters the bright realms above !

Music is but the overflow
Of heaven's full choir to man below,
Sent on some pitying angel's wing,
To teach poor mortals how to sing
Before they enter in heaven's gate,
Where blessèd spirits congregate,
And sing triumphant peans, where
They weep no more, for God is there!

HYMN FOR THE FOURTH OF JULY.

WRITTEN IN ENGLAND.

LAND of the brave and fair!
Land of the patriot's prayer!
   Our joy and pride!
Thy natal hour we sing,
And praise to God we bring,
Striking each tuneful string
   On every side!

Land of great Washington!
Down while the ages run
   His name shall live:
And in the silent thought,
While noble deeds are wrought,
And Virtue's light is sought,
   A blessing give.

Let the loud cannon roar
The joy from shore to shore,
    In loud acclaim !
Till o'er the earth is heard
The thunders of that word,
Till Liberty hath stirred
    Earth's living flame !

Fair land ! thy second birth
Shall cheer the sons of earth
    Through coming time ;
Shall lead the Nations on,
Till Liberty is won,
And man is proved a son
    Of the Divine !

Father of all ! to Thee
Our highest praise shall be !
    Thy sway we own :
The blessings of each hour,
The Nation's precious dower,
Are workings of Thy power ;
    Thy gifts alone.

GROWING OLD.

I'M growing old, and yet not very old ;
I still am dreaming of life's precious gold !
Of streams and fountains, woods and shaded
      rills ;
Of joyous rambles on the verdant hills ; —

Of sinless love, of love that could not sin,
Because the turbid waters come not in
The silver stream when the high banks o'erflow,
Giving fresh beauty where its waters flow.

Still dreaming of the merry sparkling eye,
That made the sombre shadows quickly fly,
And filled my soul with present bliss, till I
Would not believe those joys *could* ever die !

And yet 'tis not a dream that Fancy weaves ;
For I can turn and turn the lucid leaves,
As vivid as the meteor's flight, and see
The lovely form that drank its bliss with me !

The earth is silent, and the pale, bright moon
Peeps in the casement, and I see the bloom
Of the sweet woodbine, and the fragrant smell
Brings more than sweetness. O ! I cannot tell —

Why the dear shadow speaks not! for it moves
Graceful, as when we wandered in the groves,
Whose zephyrs now are breathing to my ear
The soothing sounds they bring from the blest
        sphere —

Where dwells the lost one ; and now it beckons
Me away to the deep maze ! Who reckons
Time with me, must look beyond the shining
Of the sun's rays — in the cloud's silver lining !

It beckons still ! and on I press my way,
Till Death's soft night ushers me into day,
Where the flowers bloom that die not ; and again
We'll sing together the sweet, joyous, strain —

The strain of love, that man in feebleness
Singeth to Beauty in her youthful dress !
The heart will ache ; but he who feeds its fires,
Gives blesséd visions, which the soul inspires !

Gives hope, and faith, and fancy's finest sense,
Felt in love's purest passion, parted hence ;
And time may steal the past, but it shall bring
Love's riper fruits upon its speedy wing !

HANNIBAL DRAMATIQUE.

O, for a muse of fire, that shall ascend the highest heaven
of invention! — SHAKESPEARE.

HAIL, sister of the sacred Nine !
Draw from the magic, mimic mine
Of regal fancy sparkling gems,
That trickle from the comic pens
In gaudy colors, sharp and bright;
In Wit's quick flashes, full of light !
  Full of light, full of love,
  Like the distant lights above !

Then drown us in the precious pool
Of pity for the beautiful ;
Fill us with sympathetic fire,
While Passion strikes the golden wire
Of human sorrow, deep and low,
Till the rapt listeners drink the woe ;
Till man, in woman's tears, shall find
The precious hopes of human kind !
  Tragic sorrows ever
  Raise our best endeavor.

Ah, noble powers to man are given
To lift the spirit up to heaven ;
To bid him look above the sod,
And converse with his Father — God !

To lead his fellows in the way
That promiseth a better day,
A better life ; whose end shall be
The welcome of Eternity !
    How beautiful the hope
    That lifts the spirit up !

Go on, and fill this rapid age
With trophies worthy of the page
Of coming time ; for ye, perchance,
Through your strong genius shall advance, —
O, youth of Hannibal ! — your race,
In fitness for the better place,
And Inspiration's highest rage
Shall send her lessons from your stage !
    Let bigots inly cower,
    Beneath your wondrous power.

The world is full of motives ; look
On the wide, open, passing book
Of mind and matter ! holiest faith
Lies palsied 'neath old bigots' breath ;
Give her the antidote that lifts
Man's conscious knowledge to the gifts
Of Him, who fills the boundless range
Of Nature, smiling in her change :
    Eternal change ! in thee
    Our changeless hope shall be !

THE LAST TIME.

Past moments, precious hours !
Past moments, 'mid the flowers !
Past memories, O, how fleet !
How transient, but how sweet !
Like arrow sped, or beauty dead.

Murmur, O zephyrs, low,
While our sad footsteps go
From these familiar scenes,
Life's blessèd, living dreams !
Why dost thou break the dream, O Fate ?

O Memory, treasure up,
Within thy magic cup,
The precious golden past,
Now in Time's ocean cast :
When earth is still, we'll drink our fill.

O, monumental stone !
Bleak winds shall round thee moan,
And sing, " Alone ! alone ! ! "
Where we the flowers have strown :
Our ears shall long to hear the song !

Farewell, ye living pines !
Ye everlasting signs
11

Of fadeless Eden bowers,
And heavenly mansion towers !
Ye need not fear the winter near.

Ye winding walks, farewell !
How many a quiet spell
Our lingering feet have trod
In rapture on your sod !
And now we grieve these walks to leave.

Clear fountain, sparkling spray ;
We'll think, when far away,
Of thy transparent light ;
How beautiful the sight,
When colors blend, which sunbeams send !

Farewell, fond ebon Night !
Each distant, sparkling light
Hath listened to the sigh
By angels borne on high,
And placed above, in realms of love !

It lives a floweret there,
Beyond Earth's cankering care,
Where beauty, bright and fair,
Blooms in the holy air !
There love shall roam in her own home !

ELMWOOD CEMETERY, DETROIT.

Spirits of the sylvan shades !
Often as the daylight fades
I will seek thy silent grots, —
Seek the unfrequented spots, —
Dimpled valleys, fresh and green,
Hiding from the sunset sheen,
Like the maiden in the grove,
Shrinking as she tells her love ! —

Shrinking from the eager light
Glowing in his eye so bright !
'Mid the happy solitude,
Where no listener doth intrude,
Ardent as the sunbeams are,
On the lovely form so fair,
When the raptured lover pressed
The fair lily to his breast !

Mimic hill-sides rise and fall
In thy shades, so dear to all ;
Dear as life and death to me
Every shrub and every tree !
On thy slopes the tangled vine
Clusters round this heart of mine !
Clusters full of memories sweet,
For beneath its shades we meet !

Pillared names, of great renown,
Grandly do thy summits crown !
Proud their marble columns rise,
Pointing upward to the skies, —
Pointing upward from the sod,
To the holy hills of God !
Upward, spirit ! noble worth
Scorns the cerements of earth !

Modestly, adown thy slopes,
Rise the signs of buried hopes :
Gentle hearts have gone to rest;
Gentle hands the sods have prest ;
Fragrant flowers are nestling too,
Drinking in the gentle dew
Near the little dear one's feet,
In its painless, last retreat !

Lustily the pine doth grow,
Shading sleepers down below ;
When the north wind blows he sings
Dirges for departed kings !
When the autumn zephyr sighs,
Singeth he of tender ties !
Dearer have the loved ones grown
Since they left us, sad and lone !

Gladly — sadly — oft I tread,
Silent forest of the dead,

Thy soft walks, — for fittest there
Breathe I forth my evening prayer ;
Breathe I to the holy One —
Softly to His ear alone : —
Life and death here mingle round,
And this place is holy ground !

In thy fountain spray I view
Colors of the rainbow hue ;
Calm, away from busy strife,
Promise of the fount of life
Murmurs in my listening ear
From thy dewy spray so clear :
Thy bow of promise and bright foam
Point me to that better home !

Better home, with no more death !
No more pain from parting breath !
No more drooping, tender plants
Pining 'mid the happy haunts
Of the spirits grouped around,
Where the enrapturing harp-notes sound,
Echoing down the sloping banks,
Chorused by the shining ranks ! —

Shining ranks, forever bright,
In ineffable, full light
Of the fount of life and joy !
There the spirit doth not cloy,

But it drinketh evermore,
Fount of Life, of thy rich store !
Love and Friendship there shall dwell,
And all hearts sing, " It is well ! "

FRATERNAL LOVE.

FRATERNAL LOVE ! visible sign
Of the pure heart ! In that rich mine
Lie treasures twinkling like the stars !
That jewel in the hand of Mars,
That won fair Venus from her seat,
And placed the goddess at his feet !
Thou priceless pearl ! O, could we see
This sad, sad world striving for thee !

Thou purest One ! to thy fond breast,
God's little ones were fondly prest ;
The sisters' cries, the widows' tears,
Moistened thine eyes ; thy listening ears
Drank in the sorrowing tide which flows
From human wrongs and human woes ;
And thy kind lips dropped gentlest dew,
To mould the human heart anew.

How long, thou laboring world, how long
Ere the full harmony of song,

Shall flow and echo, far and wide,
Like Earth's free air and Ocean's tide ?
O ! never yet, since angels sang
That loving song, " Good will to Man ! "
Has the grand chorus echoed back
Its music through the starry track.

How long, O God ! before thy plan
Shall give a brotherhood to man ?
Make all Earth's sons thy chosen race ;
Fraternal love on every face ;
And brothers' woes, and brothers' tears,
Find none but sympathizing ears ?
When hoarded millions cease to rise
To vex the Holy One ? whose eyes —

Pass them not by (the haughty crew),
Whose proud eyes lifted, scarcely view
The toiling millions, without hope,
'Mid the oppressor's hordes, to cope
Successful for life's common boon ;
And the wide world hath scarcely room
To give each son a tranquil spot,
For lucre blights the common lot.

Religious forms, and codes of state,
Do not avert the common fate ;
The ermine and the sacred gown
Bring not the promised blessing down ;

For that upholds the ancient way,
And this must please the rich and gay ;
One talketh learnedly and long ;
The other whines, and winks at wrong.

Both bound by custom, lucre, place,
To feed and fatten on the race ;
Both teach contentment, thus to bind
The burdens tighter on mankind ;
Both flatter, with a visor'd face ;
Both wink at wrong, and boast of grace :
While one doth wield the oppressor's rod,
The other thunders like a God !

The sacred canon passeth by
The "postern of a needle's eye ;"
And Dives smiling, looks around
Where Lazarus crawls upon the ground ;
While mansions, tall and stately, rise
For rich men, 'neath the smiling skies,
The poor must still, as ever, wait
With dogs, around the rich man's gate.

Ye bards of free and fearless verse !
Who dare the wrongs of man rehearse,
(For Freedom, since the ancient time,
Hath dwelt among the sacred Nine ;)
Raise your bold numbers, and proclaim
Your burden ! — like the ancient flame

That burneth ever warm and bright
With sons of song, — "The human right!"

Freedom and love, and holy song,
Shall yet redress each human wrong!
Religion, reason, justice, yet
Shall bounds to pride and lucre set;
And in this world of busy strife
Shall the great boon of human life
Be fetterless, and Man shall see
In each a Brother, just and free!

IMMOBILIA.

List! — what think ye of the ages?
    Can ye stop their onward flight?
And what think ye of the wages
    Of the suffering sons of light?
Would ye bind them where ye find them?
Seek ye sorrow for the morrow,
    Such as fed Oppression's night?

Listen to the passing warning:
    Hear ye not the smothered sigh?
Darkest night brings sudden morning
    To the waiting prophet's eye!
Can ye lengthen, can ye strengthen
Bygone darkness, O ye heartless?
    Gloat ye while Wrong's victims die?

Doth it make your pleasures sweeter
   Viewing brothers' wrongs and woes?
Do your cloudy hours pass fleeter
   In the murmuring blast that blows?
Heed the thunder, ere ye wonder
At the ruin that is brewing
   For the strongest tree that grows!

Must the song of Bethlehem slumber
   (Buried 'neath the passing years)
Till each heavenly, loving number
   Comes alone in sobs and tears?
O, ye mountains, loose your fountains!
Haste to borrow Earth's long sorrow,
   Till the better time appears!

Sons of Fortune, ye are sleeping
   While the torrent sweeps along!
Millions of your race are weeping
   While ye sing the siren song:
Time is flying, men are dying!
See God's finger, while ye linger,
   Pointing to Earth's waiting throng!

COMBINATION.

Men of labor; men of thought; men of skill;
Wake from your slumbers! bid tyrants be still!
Place shoulder to shoulder; march out in one line;
And this be your motto : " We all will combine ! "

How long, do you think, could your masters hold out,
'Mid their sports, and their vile dissipation, and
    gout,
If ye would but march in one resolute line,
With your flag on the breeze, and the watchword,
    " Combine " ? !

How long will ye work for the bread of to-day,
While idlers shall turn from their door-steps away
Your sons and your daughters? Come, march in one
    line,
With the flag up aloft, and your watchword,
    " Combine " !

Say, men of the hammer, — come, tell me, I pray,
Why work ye for less than ten dollars a day?
Your limbs soon grow old, and then you must pine
In weakness and want, unless you combine.

Why wait for the rich to come to your aid?
Will they give your children their clothing and
    bread?

No, no ! O, march forward, come, march in one line ,
With music and banners, and shouting " Combine " !

Ask Nature to whom should her treasures belong —
To the sloth, or industrious hand of the strong ?
For whom should the rubies and diamonds shine ?
And she answers, " To those who both work and
    combine."

Say, sons of the poor, why should you not stand
On a par with the sons of the rich in our land ?
Why bow down your heads in your beauty and prime
To the owners of wealth ? Wake up, and combine !

How long could their ships and their steamers
    sail on,
With their pride and their wealth, if your labor
    was gone ?
Their wealth would all sleep 'neath the rocks of
    the mine
If your labor should cease : then awake and combine !

They say, in their pride, " Cobbler, stick to your
    last ; "
And with Obloquy's finger, insultingly cast
Their gibes and their jeers.   Let this be a sign
To rouse you to thought, and make you combine !

Ye boast of your freedom in this our dear land :
Then why not demand for the work of your hand

An ample return ?   O, rest not supine,
But swell the grand chorus, " We all will combine ! "

Come, work for yourselves ; to each other be true ;
Nor trust in the rich, whatever ye do :
They always betray, though their words may be fine :
Ye must trust in each other, and haste to combine !

Bring your sons and your daughters, wherever ye
    meet ;
Let your hearts join as one, and your union be sweet ;
Come with music and mirth, with your footsteps
    keep time,
While the chorus rings forth, " We'll forever Com-
    bine ! "

WASHINGTON'S BIRTHDAY.

TWENTY-SECOND OF FEBRUARY.

Hail, sacred day ! auspicious morn !
When Liberty's fair Child was born ! ··
Flow on forever, gently lave
Thy banks, Potomac ! let thy wave
Glide gently down the flowery plains,
Where song-birds chant the dulcet strains :
O Eagle, hold thy banner high
Above the storm, beneath the sky,

And look below, and all around,
For far beneath thy gaze is found
Fair Independence ; and thy boast
Is heard on east and western coast :
And in the cheerful, peaceful song,
We bless the name of WASHINGTON !

Not his the proud invader's name ;
Not his the bloody tyrant's fame :
His boast was not " the scourge of God ; "
His lance was not the despot's rod —
When he was born, the angels sang,
" Rejoice, O Earth ! an honest man
Is yours to-day ! "   His body sleeps
Beneath the dew, that gently weeps
A Nation's tears ;. and gently sigh
The moaning zephyrs passing by :
And dear Potomac floweth nigh
The sacred relics where they lie —
— A Nation's boast, a Nation's pride !
'Twas here he lived, and loved, and died;
'Twas here his feet first pressed the sod ;
And here he sought his Father — God !

Columbia, weep no more your dead !
His noble spirit only fled
Your mortal vision !   He no more
Is seen upon this earthly shore :
But he still lives, and from above
Inspires the nations with his love :

Still looketh down on us below,
And bids a blessèd influence flow
Adown all time : — till king and slave
Are buried in one common grave.
Then welcome ! welcome ! be our song,
O Natal Day, to WASHINGTON !

THE MARTYR.

HE stands amid the storm a beacon light ;
  Impending clouds threaten his lifted head ;
Vile, hissing scorn, like howling winds of night,
  Fall on the ears of men with doubt and dread.

Dark ignorance, and imitation's slave,
  Cluster around him like a mighty pall ;
But with his wand of truth, and spirit brave,
  He breaks the centuried adamantine wall !

Earth shrinks in fear ! hell hurls her lurid hate !
  Systems and laws in silent terror lie !
The sculptured pillars of old custom shake !
  And falsehood's lessons shrink, and pine, and die.

O Tasso ! sing of thy Jerusalem !
  Sing of a Godfrey, and a Richard brave !
Thy heroes might not touch the garment's hem
  Of him who dies for truth, and frees the slave.

Smile not upon him, ye who pander low
  To human passions : he doth live above
Your transient lusts. Poor souls, how can ye know
  The spirit's pleasures that doth live on love ?

And would ye immolate his life to hate
  Because ye cannot grasp the golden fruit ?
The worm is but the child of stubborn fate,
  And cannot sing to sweet Apollo's lute !

How calm he sings when discords loudly roar !
  How bright his eye when charming serpents
      sing !
He on the mountain-eagle's wings shall soar,
  Above the crawling reptile's venomed sting !

Hail, Martyr of th' historic ancient time !
  The smallest bird may now your praises sing ;
Hatred and scorn, and cruel death were thine ;
  The phœnix flew to heaven on flaming wing !

Hail, warrior of to-day ! the bitter strife
  Is but the thorny road to just renown :
The poisoned dart shall pierce thee, but thy life
  Waits calmly for the sparkling, jewelled crown !

A CROCHET NEEDLE.

DEAR little friend! idle, sad, and alone!
Those dear, deft fingers forever are gone:
Nimble and swift were the motions you made
'Ere the sweet owner in silence was laid.

Weaving and tatting, so cunning and quick,
Like a magician with juggling trick,
Fashioning thoughts into beautiful flowers,
To float, and to wave in the sweet sunny hours!

Making a border for baby's new dress;
Weaving a bow for a beautiful tress;
Fashioning something for sister's sweet face;
Draping her bosom with beauty and grace!

Hanging a wreath on the dear mirror there,
That mimicked her face, so laughing and fair!
Edging the soft, downy pillow of snow,
Where the long ringlets would gracefully flow.

Thou valueless instrument, scarcely seen
By the stranger, who knew not thy mistress, I
     ween;
But the relics of those we love seem to bring
Their forms to our hearts on Memory's wing!

12

And may not the hands that clasped thee when here
Have left a sweet impress, so silent and dear
To those who remain? and a blessing bestow
To the loving ones watching and waiting below?

And may not the spirits in heaven above
Sometimes linger near the dear friends that they
　　love,
And sanctify to them the things of the earth,
And make them, than gold, more precious in worth?

I prize thee, sweet trifle, as part of the past;
A sun-ray on Memory's horoscope cast;
A plume from the wing of the bird that has flown;
And plant thee where love and its sorrow hath
　　grown!

———◆———

GOD.

FOUNT of all Being! Light of every Star!
　　Unfathomed Ocean! measureless Expanse!
Brighter than all the constellations are!
　　Thy Law is all supreme o'er time and chance.

The oceans roar, and lash their furious waves!
　　The lightnings flash, and thunders roll along!
The pent volcano frets, and fumes, and raves!
　　All are but motes in Thy harmonious song!

The nations worship at Thy sentient shrine,
 And call thee Jove, or Josh, or Allah great; —
I AM, — JEHOVAH ! — every name is thine
 That knows no present, past, or future state !

Vast, boundless circle ! distant and profound !
 Minute and viewless centre, all in all !
Comets and suns revolve the endless round ;
 And like the insect at Thy feet they fall.

Silence and solitude, and sombre night ;
 Bright, flaming, burning suns, and endless day,
Are parts of the same central Source of light ;
 And in its distant circle endless play.

Informing Spirit ! life of every soul !
 From the small moth, to angels in their flight ;
Corporeal Being ! from the sands that roll,
 To suns and planets, in their sparkling height.

Centres and shining spheres are but the dust
 Upon the floor of Thy divine abode !
And chainless ether but the yielding crust
 That bathes the boundless, blesséd hills of God !

O, finite Mind ! thou art the highest star
 That soars and sings beneath the central blaze ;
Thou measurest worlds and systems up afar,
 Within thy searching, wondering, distant gaze !

And yet how small thy mimic feeble powers,
   Compared to Him, who rules the endless round !
As dew-drops to the ocean, or as flowers,
   Compared to the bright sun, with rays profound.

Thou distant Sun ! yet ever closely nigh
   Each soul that lives within thy loving beams,
Thy spirit breathes in every sorrowing sigh,
   And gladdens all things in its solar streams !

We cannot know Thee ; we can only see
Some rays of light from Thy divinity ;
As the gay warbler takes his garments on
With borrowed plumage from the distant sun.

O, mighty Mind ! Author and Friend of all !
   We cannot comprehend Thee ; but we give
To Thee our praise, and upon Thee we call
   To help us, as *in* Thee, *like* Thee to live !

REST.

Dear Rest, we sigh, and wait to see
The murmuring streams that sing of thee.
The toiling hours and steps of pain
Mock at our hopes, and call them vain :

We labor 'neath the noontide heat,
And run the race with weary feet;
We share a brother's heavy load,
Who halts and tarries on the road;
And in the soul's unselfish love,
Where'er we stay, where'er we rove,
A brother's woe, a sister's tear,
In love and sadness bring us near.

'Tis sweet to cast a lucid ray
Of sunshine on the traveller's way;
And when dark midnight clothes him round
In the black pall, intense, profound —
— To whisper to his listening ear
Substantial sympathy and cheer;
But in this world, where faith and trust
Lie prostrate in the pool of lust,
The earnest soul, not understood,
Grows sad and weary doing good;
While senseless pomp, in proud array,
Passes the jocund hours away.

The sluggard takes his daily food,
Prepared by his industrions brood,
And whiles the lazy time away,
That circumscribes life's listless day:
The earthworm trails in slime and dust,
And human vampires live in lust,
Dragging down from its native skies
The finest bird of Paradise;

Gazing upon its pluméd wing
Unmoved, to hear it sweetly sing ;
Charming its heart with eyes of fire,
Till faint and wounded it expire ;
Bleeding, and struggling, and distressed,
It panting faints, and sinks to rest.

But cease thy murmurs, child of woe :
While human passions ebb and flow,
While time creeps on with silent tread,
When tears have flown, and love lies dead ;
When Death has snatched thy pearl away,
And thou beholdest silent lay
The casket ; — cease, O, cease to weep !
It is the calmest, sweetest sleep :
That brow is now no more opprest, —
Of all its slumbers this is best !
That heart no more in sadness bleeds
For sin and sorrow while it pleads ;
Those quiet feet no more shall start
At Slander's tongue or Envy's dart ;
Those fixéd eyes no more shall turn
From scenes where Hate and Vengeance burn.

That tongue, that soothed thy weary hours,
Is heard no more in earthly bowers ;
Those fingers, rigid now, and still,
No more thy leaping blood shall thrill ;
And the firm love that filled that breast,
That now in withered flowers is drest,

Shall swell no more its orbéd bound,
Nor answering love shall clasp it round ;
That palsied tongue no more shall chime
Love's welcome home in sweetest rhyme !

But listen, O my soul ! and hear,
Wafted on evening's zephyrs near,
The faintest murmurings, soft and sweet,
From angels whispering in their sleep ; —
— Proclaiming, in the fragrant bowers,
On clustered beds of yielding flowers,
Soft words, and low, alone for thee, —
Love's thrilling dream of prophecy !

They have found rest, — the good and true, —
And love's evangel shall renew ;
While o'er the stormy sea of life,
Thy bark sails on amid the strife ;
And when the fire-clad clouds are riven,
Reveal some glimpses of their heaven !

Labor and love, O child of earth !
For life's revealing gleams are worth
More than thy toils ; and soon shall rise
Thy fadeless mansion in the skies !
And thou, a child to glory born,
Shalt enter on life's second morn,
More glad than bird at opening day,
That bathes him in the sun's first ray !

And sweeter shall thy spirit sing,
Than warbled notes in early spring !
A happier song shall greet thee there,
Than in sweet summer fills the ear,
When the rapt lark mounts to the sun,
And trills his welcome orison !
For though like thine his soul may rise,
In the high archway of the skies,
Thou art the heir of endless mirth,
While he falls backward to the earth !

Love cannot die ! though darkness fall
Around the soul, like Egypt's pall :
Love cannot die ! though Winter's blast,
Its freezing mantle o'er it cast :
Love cannot quench ! though tempests pour
Their cataracts of water o'er :
Love cannot cease ! though death shall creep
Into the heart, and still its beat :
Love shall not lose her natal star,
Though in the heavens it mounts afar !
But when the weary race is won,
Mingle her fires, and shine as one !
Love cannot stain her spotless robe
With retrogression's cumbrous load ;
And would not call from realms of bliss
Its souls to dwell in homes like this :
Dear Love ! it cannot dwell alone :
Though out beyond the farthest zone

Its object dwell, there is a way,
More lucid than the sun's bright ray,
On the electric wave of thought,
Where Love's quick messages are brought;
And Love her sweetest victory sings
While her own messages she brings !

Rest, rest at last ! Is this not rest,
To sleep upon the loved one's breast?
To feel the breath of fragrant gales
Wafting and wooing with a kiss,
The weary soul, to realms of bliss ! ?
Is this not rest, when quickened sight
Beholds the messengers of light ! ?
Is this not rest, while over thee
Thy angels bend in ecstasy ! ?
Is this not rest, to lay thy head
Upon Love's couch, soft pillowéd ! ?
To see the form that long had fled
Bend o'er thee on the nuptial bed ! ?
Is it not rest, to hear them say,
" Come, weary one, from earth away ! ? "
To see them point to landscapes wide,
Beyond the dreamy, silent tide,
Where far and near thy eyes behold
The emerald floor, with flowers of gold !
Where rainbows span the endless round,
And bells of silver deck the ground,
Inmixed with pearls that grow and chime
Nature's soft song of endless rhyme !

Where streamlets murmur, all day long,
Strains sweeter than Earth's sweetest song !
Where fear no more starts at the sound
Of lurking foes, that linger round ;
But like the perfume of the rose,
Sweet, loving trust forever flows !
Where beauty lives, and grows more fair,
For waste and sorrow come not there ;
Where changeless love more bright shall shine
Than sparkling gems in Nature's mine ;
Where Love, in her own flowers, is drest ; —
This, O my soul, this, this is Rest !

MATER.

Name of all Names !   O, how I love
To think thee nigh where'er I rove !
To feel thy breath upon my cheek ;
To hear thy lingering accents speak ;
To know that thou dost love me yet,
Tenderly, as when last we met ;
Firmly, as when I took my rest,
Securely, on thy loving breast !

Centre of Home ; Fountain of Life !
Its solace in the ceaseless strife ;

Its cooling shade from noontide heat;
Its covert, when the tempests beat :
Its quiet place of sweet repose ;
Its garden, where the love-flower grows :
Its echoing thought, when words are dear ;
Its angel, when the heavens appear !

Often in slumber I do seem
To see thee in the midnight dream ;
To hear thy cautious footsteps nigh,
As when thou sing'st my lullaby :
To feel thy tender hand on mine,
And hear thee whisper, " I am thine ! "
Ah, I am thine, though time hath shed
Its sprinkled snow-flakes on my head !

Yes, I am thine, though tempest-tost
On life's rough waves, yet never lost ;
Thine, in temptation's blackest night;
Thine, when false friendship takes its flight ;
Thine, when my tears like raindrops flow ;
Thine, when all pleasures fail below :
When Fortune's favors cease to shine,
My heart still sings, " Thou, thou art mine ! "

Mysterious bond, that Nature gives ;
Affection's tie forever lives !
The eye may fade, the cheek grow pale ;
E'en Memory's magic page may fail : —

The form may bend beneath its load,
And footsteps stumble on the road;
The soul may beat its cage of clay,
But love shall bear it safe away!

Ye sons of sorrow, weep no more!
Behold, on yonder spirit shore
The loved ones dwell! nor think that they
Forget, in realms of endless day,
Their toiling children left behind;
No! sweet Affection, ever kind,
Descends to earth, unseen by thee,
And soothes away thy agony!

Dear Mother! sad misfortunes lower,
On every step in life's dark hour;
And mirth is short, and peace takes wing,
When War and Passion's curséd din
Clashes and foams like lurid flame!
But thou forever art the same:
Still doth thy fadeless love increase,
And in my soul thou singest "Peace!"

Words cannot paint, or half express
Affection's thoughts, that ever press
Upon the soul. Ah, no! they dwell
Forever there, a precious spell!
Like the sweet fragrance of the rose,
Which on each gentle zephyr flows,

Ever unseen, but ever there,
A sweet breath on the desert air!

A Mother's love! 'tis sweet to sing
Of Nature's budding, opening spring!
'Tis sweet to sing of summer flowers,
Of sparkling dew and freshening showers;
Of wooing winds and spicy gales,
That kiss the lover and his sails;
Of the sweet nectarine's painted face,
And all the pleasing landscape trace.

And when fair Autumn speeds along,
With joy we listen to its song —
— Its song of plenty; golden-sheaves,
And ripening fruits, and changing leaves;
'Tis then our grateful raptures swell,
And on life's richest bounties dwell:
But sweeter, deeper, and above
All else, swells up a Mother's love!

Farewell, dear Mother! on thy sod
I often kneel, and pray to God!
Ah! 'tis so peaceful kneeling there
To offer up my evening prayer!
So calm beside thy turf to lie,
And feel 'tis beautiful to die!
So sweet to linger there and rest,
And dream of sleeping on thy breast!

Farewell, farewell ! but not to thee ;
Farewell to Sorrow's minstrelsy :
Welcome, O Faith, and angel sight !
Welcome, O Love, forever bright !
Farewell, sad Earth, when she shall say,
" Come from thy sorrows, come away ! "
Welcome, O Death, for thou shalt bring
Mother and heaven upon thy wing !

REMINISCENCE.

Sweet Ella, dear, my heart is sad,
    While Memory tells of thee :
I'm thinking of thy loving smile,
    So precious still to me.

The years have passed so lonely by,
    The seasons come and go ;
The sunlight glistens on the dew,
    And lightens all below ; —

But this lone heart cannot rejoice
    With Nature all around,
And in the sun's all-cheering rays
    No light for me is found.

The moonbeams lie upon the lake,
  In silver-spangled gleams ;
While all the stars in silence sleep,
  And wander in their dreams.

I wonder if they dream of thee,
  Within their yielding beds ?
If they had known thee when alive,
  They'd dream of thee when dead !

I dream : and dream that I would dream
  Forever of my love !
I dream that she is looking down
  Upon me from above.

I dream : but no, I cannot tell
  If it be all a dream ; —
I dream I see thy lovely form
  In fields of fadeless green !

I dream I hear thy gentle voice ;
  'Tis Music's sweetest spell !
Bathing my soul in its dear tones,
  That sing, — " All, all is well ! "

I dream thy love is ever true,
  E'en though thy footsteps tread
The flowery paths of Paradise,
  By angel wardens led !

For every flower that greets thy eye
    Shall bring my love to mind ;
And soon adown those flowery plains
    My spirit thou shalt find.

Thy mortal presence was a dream,
    So short, so sad, so sweet !
But death shall never more divide,
    When we again shall meet !

Alone and sad, this heart of mine
    Still wanders here below,
And waits impatient for the hour
    When it to thee shall go.

Who loveth once, forever loves,
    Nor time, nor space divide :
And true love cannot rest content
    Till love sits by her side.

Forget me not amid your joys ;
    Down 'mid the fields of space,
Is not your land of love and light
    A higher type of this ?

And what to you and I
    Is life, with all its outside forms ?
It is the soul that ever lives,
    And every place adorns.

Love, like a star, all space around
   Enlivens with its rays ;
And in life's darkest hour it most
   Delights our anxious gaze !

And thus thy love shall ever flow
   Down through the endless time,
And bless me with its constant glow,
   And make thee ever mine !

And like Prometheus, I will rise
   Above the tortured hour,
And claim thee as love's precious prize —
   My fadeless, fragrant flower !

SPIRITUAL ANNIVERSARY SONG.

Joy to the world ! Ye angels bring
Glad inspirations while we sing !
No hero's praise we here rehearse ;
No warrior's name adorns our verse ;
No fulsome peans swell the lay,
That ushers in this sacred day.
No massive palace doors unfold,
To fill our eyes with gems and gold ;
No jewelled crown or glittering spear
Bringeth our willing footsteps here.

13

Not Fashion's sons or daughters stand
Around the bard, on either hand.
No hierarchs, of ancient date,
With sanctimonious pride of state,
Lead in our songs, or chant aloud
Their unknown jargon to the crowd.
No bigots bend in holy fear,
With prostrate form, and senseless tear :
No hypocritic Pharisee
Says, " I am holier far than thee ! " —
" Poor, erring man ! "   No ; here we meet,
All children, at the Father's feet.
Here our glad hearts forever burn
With strong desire, to love and learn !

O, Fountain on yon spirit shore,
Sparkling and flowing evermore !
Sweet Fountain, falling from above,
Filling our hearts with endless love !
O, ample River of our God !
Adown your banks our feet have trod
With loved ones, who have passed away,
And dwell in cloudless realms of day :
And often from the other shore,
Their cheerful voices call us o'er ;
They often leave the mansions fair,
And to our sorrowing hearts repair,
To bring us hope, to lead us on,
Through the rough paths that they have gone.

To give us patience on our way,
And point us to a brighter day !
To shed a sacred influence round,
Where waiting, loving hearts are found.
O, come ye blessed ! come to-day,
And call our silent thoughts away, —
Away from sorrow, and from sin ;
Come to our hearts and enter in ;
Bring wisdom from your happy sphere,
To guide us while we linger here ;
So that each passing, earthly day,
Shall scatter jewels on its way :
So that some sorrowing hearts that mourn
In life's rough road, to us may turn,
And see the sympathizing tear,
And words of comfort ever hear :
May feel the open, generous hand,
That aids their faltering feet to stand.

Open your doors, ye angels bright,
And pour on us a flood of light !
Show your dear faces, press our hands ;
Smile on us in our circled bands ;
Sing your sweet songs, for when ye come,
Ye bring us heaven, ye bring us home !
O, send us from your realms above
A mother's presence, and her love ;
A father's wisdom, brave and strong,
To choose the right and flee the wrong ;

And may the fount of wisdom glow
In all our hearts, that we may know
Fair truth from error, and arise,
With Virtue, to her native skies !

Hail, brothers, hail ! we only wait
The swinging of the crystal gate !
Fight bravely, fight for truth and right,
And Victory's crown shall greet your sight !
Fair sisters, welcome with your love !
Its full fruition is above ;
There ye shall bathe in its bright beams,
And drink its overflowing streams !

No sombre rites their sadness shed ;
They come not here, — we have no dead.
And Science sings her cheerful lays
To Immortality's high praise !
The world is ours, for round its zone
Departed spirits find a home :
This world is ours, for unseen powers
Keep vigils through the endless hours :
They watch and wait ; they lift the veil,
And sigh and sing in every gale.
They speak in flowers and verdant sod,
And point men upward to their God !
They fill the seer's enraptured sight,
And bathe the mourner's soul in light !
They show their faces, as of yore,
And " Auld Lang Syne " they sing us o'er ;

They bring the ancient artists nigh,
And quick as shadows passing by,
Present to our astonished gaze
The forms we loved in other days !
They ope the ears of mortal men,
And give their fond words back again ;
And through our tears they make us sing,
" Fair angel Death, thou hast no sting ! "

Roll on, ye planets ! grandly roll,
O children, of the central soul !
Burn on, ye suns ! reflect His light,
And sing forever of His might !
Float on, O Ether ! bathe them round
On your soft bosom ; take the sound
From star to star, from sun to sun ;
And bid the angel heralds run
Down through the endless fields of space,
To mortal men of every race,
To sing the welcome song of peace
And harmony, till discord cease.
To raise the grovelling sons of earth
To joy that springs from second birth ;
To fill their souls with holy love,
Like Nature and the hosts above !
To make us more than heroes here,
And bring our loving angels near.
O, mother Nature ! oft as I gaze
Out on thy works, my soul with praise

And adoration calmly sings,
And to her heart Love's spirit brings,
Till lost in her great sea of bliss,
She leaps for joy, and shouts, O this,
Ay, this is life ! and soars above
The toils of earth, to realms of love !

Bring songs of joy, and fragrant flowers ;
This day, O mortals, this is ours !
Glad angels, in celestial bowers,
Echo the song, " 'Tis ours ! 'tis ours !
And soon the chorus shall resound,
Wherever loving hearts are found,
From earthly homes and spirit towers,
" This bridal day is ours, 'tis ours ! "

CHRISTMAS.

HAIL, Holy Child ! sweet tenant of the manger !
Long centuries rolling on, welcome the stranger
In each Christmas gift, each loving, kindred thought
That swells the breast of childhood.   O, happy lot,
To be a favored child !   The young heart boundeth
Like the fleecy innocent, that roundeth
The verdant hill-sides, singing its baby note
To her who calleth in the grassy slope.

Ah, children, He of Galilee was poor ;
The costly palace opened not its door
To Joseph's Child, when Mary, sad and lonely,
Presented₊to the earth the best, the only
Gift that shall endure an everlasting joy ;
And angels sang sweet peans to her Boy !
Sing, little children, sing your Christmas song !
Lift up the poor ; bid *them* your strains prolong !

A brighter day is coming on the earth :
Though slow its footsteps, yet the happy birth
Of Him who blessed the children, and whose arms
Embraced them, with his pure and holy charms,
Shall fill the souls of men with sweet fraternal love ;
And the world's people, like the hosts above,
Shall drink the living waters, flowing down
From the supernal throne, and wear the fadeless
    crown !

Haste, happy day ! fling odors on the blast
That moaneth to the coming time the past ; —
The terrible past, red with the bloody gore
That flowed from noblest hearts ! and to the poor
Give joy and gladness ; to the pure in heart
Give peace ; give visions full of glory ; part
The dense curtain that divides the distant scene,
And bless Earth's millions with the prophet's dream !

MY FLOWER GARDEN.

My Garden is sweet ; in the valley it lies,.
　Where the frog, and the whippoorwill sings ;
'Mong its flowers and its shrubs the humming-bird
　　　• flies,
　Sipping nectar, and sunning his wings !

The Rose blushes there with its petals so sweet,
　'Neath the gaze of the warm wooing sun ;
It hides 'neath the green leaves, but often doth peep
　Up to heaven, while he journeys along !

The Violet drinks in the dew and the breeze,
　And hangeth her meek little head ;
Not daring to gaze on the tall spreading trees,
　But reclines in her beautiful bed !

The Dahlia is there, in her various hues,
　Like a queen in the garden, I ween ;
Her colors more bright than the full fragrant rose ;
　On the surface her beauty is seen.

The pure, milk-white Lily breathes sweet on the air,
　Like a bride in her chamber of love !
Like sweet silver bells, swing her petals so fair,
　Keeping time to the songs in the grove !

The Woodbine looks up to the shrub that is nigh,
　Reaching out for his wide-spreading arms ;
O, she seeketh a place for her blossoms to lie,
　Like sweet babes, in their beautiful charms !

The Primrose peeps out, like a star in the sky,
　From the soft mossy bank near the rill ;
And the honey-bee kisses her mild yellow eye,
　While of sweetness he drinketh his fill !

O, countless and fair are the flowers that I love,
　And sparkling their dew-drops are seen !
Come, roam with me there, for wherever we rove,
　Nature smiles in her garments of green !

EVENING.

CALM Evening ! who but loveth thee ?
'Tis in thy tranquil hours we see
The distant lights ; Infinity
Spreads out her far-extending plains,
Traversed by angels, whose sweet strains,
Far as the mighty Maker reigns —

— Float on forever ! and each bird
That singeth gladly, sure hath heard
Some distant sonnet, that hath stirred

His quivering accents, and his song
Doth but some spirit-strain prolong
To mortal ears, by mortal tongue!

Thy ebon curtain hideth not
The heavenly vision ; for each spot
Reveals the unfathomed, mighty plot
Of Nature's labyrinth to each eye,
That contemplates the illumined sky,
Where Wisdom's shining wonders lie.

Fair Evening! mortal eye hath seen
No regal monarch like thy queen !
No crown like hers has ever been
Placed on Earth's princes, for each gem
That fills the monarch's diadem
Is sparkling dust beneath her train !

Well may the ardent lover gaze
On her whose light around him plays,
Revealing that belovéd face
In bashful beauty, that hath spread
Youth's blessed dreams around his bed,
And Virtue's purest influence shed !

Dream on in her soft, holy light !
Too soon those moments take their flight ;
Too soon shall come that sombre night,
Whose shadows hasten from afar
To hide from view thy spirit-star,
Down where the dust and ashes are !

And then, O Evening! then shall he
That star in all its beauty see!
But, O, too high its light shall be!
Too far from him, who oft did kiss,
With thrilling ecstasy of bliss!
Ah! it was all for death and this!

O Father! 'mid the evening prayer,
Breathe softly, in the evening air,
"Peace, spirit! she is living there!
O, dry the tear: the soul hath fled,
Far from the dwellings of the dead,
Up where celestial visions spread!"

The blazing orb of day may rise
With mighty grandeur in the skies;
But in the evening sacrifice
The listening fond one hears the sound
Of loving footsteps lingering round,
Where Friendship's constant feet are found.

Let madness tempt the midnight hour,
Where pomp and pride destroy the flower
Of youth, gaining the deadly dower
Of Dissipation; but the wise,
By observation, sweetly rise
To those grand heights where folly dies!

Where God is seen, supreme, alone!
Where scintillations from His throne
Lie sparkling on each planet's zone!

There songs of joy are ever heard,
Chanting the praises of that Word,
Forever blesséd and adored !

———◦◦◦———

TRUST.

Sweet Trust! O, couldst thou ever live
    Within the human soul ! The child
Alone hath that prerogative —
    Its angel-heart with thee is filled !
Sleep on, O, sleep ! Thou dost not know
    The future vision ! It will come
Full soon, for time shall quickly flow :
    O, rest thee in thy tender home !

How soon the spell is broken ! look
    Not in human eyes ! ah, look not !
For they are not the spirit's book
    Where thou canst read thy changing lot;
Trust not those crystal, lucid balls, —
    Their light doth swiftly pass away,
Swift as the lovely curtain falls,
    That shutteth out the light of day.

Ah, cruel fate ! he that doth live
    On human passions hath no rest ;
They promise, but they do not give
    The answer to thy aching breast ;

The jewelled casket fills thine eye
  With its bright colors, O how bright!
Uncovered — all thy hopes shall die;
  For ashes greet thy anxious sight!

Thou canst not find beneath the sun,
  O man! a changeless home of love;
Earth's choicest spirits live alone;
  They fix their constant trust above;
They know the blessèd Source, and they
  Play not with baubles here below,
But catch the beams that round them play,
  From the blest world to which they go!

Trust not the passing multitude; —
  They clamor when thy words are sweet;
Behold, along thy path are strewed
  The stones that did the martyrs greet;
Their whited sepulchres appear
  To lure thee on to high renown;
They ate the bread of sorrow here,
  And dropped the sword, to grasp the crown!

Earth is the fiery crucible
  That purifies the good man's heart;
He that the flowers of heaven would cull,
  Must feel Earth's cruel, poisoned dart!
Be tranquil, spirit; thou shalt be
  The victor when the dart is drawn ·
From thy sad heart; and thine shall be
  The rest, where bravest souls have gone.

Work on ! it is the noblest boon
 Bestowed on mortals ! work and strive ;
Doubt not thy strength ; for thou shalt soon
 Rest from thy labor, and arrive
Where work and rest alike shall be
 Thy pleasure ; and His holy will
Shall be the food that feedeth thee !
 Trust Him, O spirit ! Peace, be still !

GOING HOME.

Long years and slow ; long dream of years !
 The faded cheek, the wasted form ;
The fountain closed, whence flowed the tears,
 So copiously, in life's young morn :
  Alone, alone, I'm going home !

I'm going home ; but who can tell
 How many feet shall meet me there ?
For, O, how long the last farewell !
 How long since then the exile's prayer !
  Alone, alone, I'm going home !

My father's voice, my mother's love,
 Are hushed and gone ; forever fled
My sister's smile ; all dwell above —
 Their gentle forms are with the dead !
  Alone, alone, I'm going home !

The strangers loved the exiled boy,
  Admired his song, and joined the lay,
Partook his swelling, gushing joy !
    His tears they saw not ; — it was day :
    Alone, alone, I'm going home !

I've dwelt among them, and have given
  My strength of life, my constant toil ;
Have gloried in their growth, and striven
  For peace amid life's long turmoil.
    And now, alone, I'm going home !

I've roved amid their copses green ;
  Drank of their trickling mountain springs ;
Their many-colored flowers I've seen,
  And quaffed the joy that Nature brings !
    But now, alone, I'm going home !

Farewell, fair land ! I cannot tell
  If ever on thy sod shall press
His feet again who sings farewell !
  But know, my tongue thy name will bless,
    When all alone I reach my home !

Thou art the urn, whose breast contains
  The dust of those who gave me birth ;
O, guard those precious, fond remains,
  For they have made thee holy earth !
    And I, alone, am going home !

Dear native land ! a turf I bring
From each sad mound that marks their rest ;
And in thy bounteous, lengthened spring,
Will place them on thy verdant breast !
Sad and alone, I'm coming home !

Thy dews shall make them grow and spread ;
Thy violets shall nestle there ;
And I will watch thy grassy bed,
And press my knee in silemt prayer,
When I, alone, am safely home !

HANNIBAL.

WELL named, if named to honor him
Who menaced the world's masters !   I win
No guerdon, if I place thee not
Beside his name a worthy spot !
Thy strong, eternal hills shall stand
In beauty, firm and sure, and grand
(To grace the name that honors thee),
Fit dwellings for the good and free !

Ye dwellers on the Rhine and Maine ;
Ye chamois-hunters, from the chain
Of everlasting Alpine heights,
Whose glaciers mock the starry lights,

Hie hither to our fruitful slopes,
To drown your sorrows in the hopes
That spring and blossom in the soul,
Where Freedom crowns the happy goal!

Grand Mississippi! on thy banks
The Muse, prophetic, views the ranks
Of mingling millions, from all climes,
Producing wealth from fields and mines!
Sees brighter records for the page,
That paints the coming golden age!
Sees Commerce in her countless sails,
Laden with wealth, and spicy gales!

O, let the Tree of Knowledge rise,
And spread its branches 'neath the skies!
Crowning each summit, till the fruit
Droppeth its seeds, and taketh root
In human hearts, and planteth there
Improvement's gems, lovely and fair,
Glistening like dew-drops on the sod,
Lifting the soul up, up to God!

Then shall the courts of God be seen
Full of true worshippers, whose mien
Reflecteth back the Father's love!
And joyous songs shall float above —
Above the earth, where toil and care
Burden with sighs the good man's prayer; —

14

Above the appetites, which fill
The erring, sorrowing human will ;
Above the miser's cursèd lust,
That grovels in the shining dust :
Then Passion's dross shall pass away,
And earth behold a brighter day !

Thou sacred place, where loved ones sleep,
Where fond ones oft repair to weep !
(Beyond the fearful "Lover's Leap ") —
Thou earthly link, that binds the race
To spirits in that better place ; —
How green and peaceful dost thou lie,
Making us almost wish to die !
To die ? — to live !   Where partings cease,
Where all the loved ones dwell in peace !

Beautiful Hannibal ! our boast
Shall be of thee, on distant coast ;
And on the Seven-hilled City's dome,
We'll bless thee with the name of Home !
And thy round summits shall outvie
The loveliest smiling slopes that lie
Beneath Italia's classic clime ; —
And there my song shall call thee mine !

HELL.

SOME people doubt it : very well, —
But I believe there is a hell.
I strolled around the other night,
And saw men full of rum and fight ;
I visited a dainty dame, —
You'd like, perhaps, to know her name ; —
I'll tell you — it was " Mistress Quiz : "
And when her tongue began to whiz,
It seemed to me like a hot flame,
By passion fed ; — blasting a name
I'd known for years as good and true !
I think, kind reader, now don't you ?
That these bad men, and Mistress Quiz,
Dwell very near where Satan is !

When very young I boarded round ;
In one home happiness I found ;
But out of four-and-twenty more,
It seemed as though the head was sore,
Or the heart sick ; for, night and day,
Time passed with scarce a loving ray :
And when the hour of setting sun
Found all at home, and work all done,
It was like brawling pot-house, when
Frequent potations heat the brain ; —
For she who'd promised to obey
Her chosen love, drove him away ;

Or, if he staid, his manhood gone ;
Or worse than this, — proud and alone !

Sometimes I saw a noble wife,
Living a loving, generous life ;
Dispensing comfort all around
To others ; but, alas ! she found
No compensation for her love,
Save what was sent her from above :
He who had whispered in her ear
Promise of future love and cheer,
Gave bitter answers to her prayer;
Sought strangers, while he left her there,
A withered flower ; nor sun, nor dew
Cheered the pure heart, so kind and true !

Oft Nature's child was linked with one
Who set the iron heart upon
Earth's baubles, or its yellow dust, —
Lived like a brute, and burned with lust !
Living to leave a race behind
A *living* curse to human kind,
And to themselves sorrow and woe !
Go to the tub, and spittal go,
Ye poor unfortunates ! for who
Care for such helpless dregs as you ?
We keep the cholera far away ;
For rhinderpest we freely slay
Our hecatombs ; but lust must lie
An incubus, if millions die !

Law places where he cannot steal,
The thief, for the great common weal ;
But he who sends a liquid fire,
Transmitted from a brutish sire
To crimeless children, down and down
Succeeding years, — law doth not frown
On such ! O, why doth Justice wink
On crimes like this ! ? I really think
That wealth and honor (?) are the cause
We have not better human laws ;
For do not kings and princes stain
Earth's annals with lascivious shame ?
And is not wealth the fruitful nest
Of sin, corruption, and unrest ?
'Tis not the brightest side, I know,
Of human life ; but let that go
At present (I often love to tell
Of that), have I not proved a Hell ?

PATRIA.

In the sad, sorrowing, lengthened years,
When Time hath dried the childish tears,
And Manhood looketh fondly o'er
The golden times, which come no more ; —
There's many a tender, holy thought,
Which time and sorrow taketh not

Out from the wanderer's inmost heart,
That lingers until life depart!

We bustle in the busy crowd,
Join in its pleasures, light and loud;
Partake its projects, gain applause;
Drink in its spirit, and its cause;
Speak noble words for common weal;
Think deep and long, and freely feel
For others, till all hearts grow warm
With generous thoughts or bitter scorn.

We wander many a weary mile;
Gain knowledge, and the hours beguile
With scenes of nature and of art,
Entering, but filling not the heart;
Admire the works of mighty mind,
Left on the annals of mankind;
Eagerly trace creation o'er; —
But childhood cometh back no more!

Sometimes an aged form I see,
That bringeth dimly unto me
The tender, doting, loving eye:
And quickly, through the year gone by,
My fancy painteth every scene
Where childhood roved, 'mid pastures green;
Guided, instructed in the lore
That covers Nature's pages o'er.

Guided so tenderly, so calm,
'Mid air that breathed a fragrant balm ;
'Mid wild flowers, and the clinging vine ;
The modest jasmine, the woodbine ;
The scented clover, the blue-bell ;
The starry cowslip in the dell ;
The crocus and the violet ;
The snowdrop in my memory yet ; —

The gentlest, fairest, purest flower
That ever bloomed in Dian's bower,
Or decked the garland on the brow
Of her who made the virgin's vow :
Fair emblem of the angel love
Of those who wait for me above,
To strike with them the golden wire !
To embrace a noble, sainted sire !

Sing, loving Muse, sing of his worth !
Nature's fond child, — a noble birth
Of goodness, — seemed to ever grow
With age ; the flowing locks like snow,
Looked beautiful ; and when he could,
Benevolence, like daily food,
Dispensed he to his fellow-man ;
Then resting, like an angel sang ! —

Sang like an angel ! O, how sweet
The song when child and parent meet !

When hearts together, flowing on
In joyful strains, bid care be gone ;
Inspiring Music ! ne'er shall I
Lose thy fond spell ; sweet Harmony
Forever dwell in this sad heart,
And solace me till life depart !

Calm Sabbath mornings ! oft I dwell
On thy past scenes I loved so well ;
Thy stillness, broken by the spell
Of singing birds and matin bell,
Seemed like enchanting music sent
From heaven to our own firmament !
Thy child, my Father, still doth love
Those sounds that lift the heart above : —

Above the sensual appetites ;
Above the ceremonial rites ;
Above the bigot and his prayer ;
Above the consecrated chair ;
Above proud Fashion's menial slave ;
Above the cant, that cannot save ; —
Soon, kindest Father, I shall come
To Thee, above the starry dome !

IN MEMORIAM.

THREE years to-day, three lonely years ! —
O, vacant hours ! O, burning tears !
O, homeless heart, and restless head ! —
Since thou wast numbered with the dead !

Spring's first wild rose thy pillow prest;
The last lay on thy lifeless breast !
'Twas hard to die, for love had grown
For one whose heart was all thine own !

Thy life was gentle ; like thy voice,
It made Earth's weary ones rejoice ;
'Twas like the mountain streams, that flow
In music to the plains below !

'Twas like the sweetest bird of song,
That warbles joyous all night long,
And charms the darkest hours away,
Until appears the morning ray.

How tender, when the storm was high,
Those loving orbs would linger nigh !
How soft those fairy footsteps fell
Upon the fragrant flowery dell !

And while I gazed, to me was given
Prophetic dreams of home in heaven !
But now, I wonder, canst thou see
The flowers I plant, and pluck for thee ? !

Yes, thou art near me ! and I sit
Where often tread thy angel feet ;
And though I miss those earthly eyes,
Thou smil'st on me from Paradise !

This " muddy vesture " wrapped around
My spirit, shutteth out the sound
Of that sweet voice, or I could hear
Its cheerful accents, soft and clear !

Come often, darling ! for I need
Thy presence ; — I, a bruiséd reed,
Bending before the storm, can see
No staff to aid but God and thee.

Come often ; let thy presence fill
My spirit, till a joyous thrill
Pervades my being, and I feel
A silent gladness o'er me steal !

Could I but see thy spirit form,
Then might the wildest thunder-storm
Of earth beat on me ; and meanwhile
I'd meet it with a fearless smile !

Could thy dear voice, like gentle dew,
Fall on my ear, my memory true
To the bright past should leap for joy,
And all the present ills destroy !

But life is short in mortal form,
And night fades at approaching morn ;
And soon the spirit that has fled,
Shall with the waiting wanderer wed !

I thank thee, loved one, that thy feet
Oft visit, when I sadly weep ;
And that thy careful touch doth thrill
My soul, and I am calm and still !

Love need not write thy precious name,
Nor speak it till we meet again ;
'Tis writ in flowers that bloom above,
In the dear garden of our love !

DEATH.

" Tarry, sweet cousin Suffolk, till my soul shall fly with thine to heaven ! " — SHAKESPEARE.

THERE'S a mystic river ; 'tis dark and deep ;
The boatman's oar hath a leaden sweep ;
There's a viewless dread when its waves are felt ;
There are shifting sands where the loved have knelt.

There are locks of hair adown its shore,
And broken rings on the sandy floor ;

There are mournful sounds in the fitful breeze,
That sweep through the limbs of the leafless trees.

There are faded flowers, with their fragrance fled ;
There's a sombre pall o'er their petals of red ;
There's a burning thought on a tablet of white,
And a dove with its plumage of azure and white.

There's a tiny shoe 'neath a trundle-bed,
And the echoes sound where my footsteps tread ;
There's a little silent face on the wall,
That smiles no more at the loving call.

There's a flitting shadow, that whispers low,
Of the silent smile, 'neath the locks of snow ;
There's a distant sound in the dreamy air,
Like a shout ; — but it dies in a mournful prayer.

There's a broken heart, and a listless eye ;
The senseless laugh, and the frantic cry :
There's a doleful song, and an aimless way ;
There's a restless night, and a lifeless day.

There's a listening ear where the moonbeams fall,
And a vacant place by the garden wall ;
There's a shady bower, with a lonely seat;
There's a quivering lip, there are lingering feet.

There's a manly form, in its strength and pride,
Just taking the boat for the other side ;

There's a maiden fair, with an eye like heaven,
Still straining to see the cloud-mist riven !

There's a star through the mist, which the ages
    bring nigh,
And the boatman sings, and the shadows fly ;
There's a vision of love, and a voice through the
    gloom,
And a spirit that smiles on the flowers of the tomb.

There's a visiting band from the realms of the blest ;
There's a lullaby song from the mansions of rest ;
There's a certainty sings where but doubts moaned
    before,
And they welcome us home to the bright summer
    shore !

WITHERED LEAVES.

Out upon the woodlands, Whirling in the breeze ;
Dancing on the brook sands, Flying from the trees.

Playing with the wild flowers, Kissing them in glee,
Whispering of the past hours, Spent with busy
    bee —

Giving up the honey, When the sun was high ;
Looking up so funny, At the bright blue sky.

How it shook all over, Many a windy day,
Looking at the clover, Blossoming so gay —

Clustering all together, Beautiful and bright,
Shining like a feather, In its sunny flight —

Feather of the wild bird, Gladly soaring on ;
Beauty which the wind stirred, Gushing forth in
     song !

Floating on the river, Skimming on its breast ;
How the leaf doth shiver, Ere it goes to rest !

Beautiful as ever, In the sunset sheen,
Though the frosts have made her, Doff the youth-
     ful green.

Ere to sleep she goeth, Lovingly she sighs —
He who made us knoweth, Where the dead leaf lies.

He who loves his creatures, Takes them to his
     breast,
And the leaves are preachers, When they go to rest.

He knows when the fond hearts, Sadly go away ;
Knoweth when the tear starts, Knoweth what we
     say :

He knows how we whisper, Loving words and true ;
Knoweth how we kissed her, When we bade adieu !

Knoweth where we laid her, In the budding spring,
In the hand that made her, Where the wild birds
    sing —

Sing to her so gladly, Seeming thus to say, —
" Friends have left thee sadly, Sadly gone away —

" Knowing not thy spirit, Singeth up on high,
(Loving faith can hear it), Sweeter far than I."

Spirit, sing forever, In the happy groves !
Angel forms shall never, Leave thy last repose !

THE SABBATH.

Thou azure arch, thou limitless expanse !
Bow without end, uncircumscribed and vast !
Infolding in thy wondrous round all worlds ;
Upholding all within their spheres as firm
As adamantine columns, yet so soft
Their yielding beds, that the sweet infant smiles
When the lithe curtain plays upon its face,
And kissing gently, leaves no other trace !

Thou unseen God ! beyond, above, below ;
Beyond all worlds, above this spacious bow ;
Below the deep foundations, yet so nigh,
That all things, seen and unseen, feel the eye

Of supreme power, of boundless, peerless love ;
Smiling all day upon the sun's quick beams ;
And when the moon and stars look from above,
Opening to man the spirit's distant dreams !

O holy Sabbath ! when the orient brings
Ithuriel's flashing spear and golden wings,
To kiss the pearly dew, and bid it rise,
Like a sweet incense, to the bending skies !
O, then could man's exalted spirit fly
On the same fragrant cloud that passeth by,
With willing wings, to meet the Father — God —
What golden streams of light should gild the road!

Without thy rest, O Sabbath ! it were vain
To bid Improvement lead its smiling train !
For what are wealth and science, when the mind,
To drudging labor, is for aye confined ?
But in this rest man feels he is above
All that he sees, and feels the fount of love
Flowing in copious streams into his heart,
Infusing springs that never shall depart !

Then every flower delights his gazing eye,
And every distant planet cometh nigh ;
And both alike sing to his raptured soul,
Sounds sweet as angel harps in that blest goal
Of endless Sabbath, where they ever sing
The joyous notes with the young cherubim !
Sing to His praise who saw His works were good, —
Who spake the word, and all creation stood !

MY SISTER.

SLEEP, sister! It is past; the agony
Is over, and we will not weep for thee.
Thy life was lovely, and so sweet thy words
To thy young brother's ear, the little birds
Listened to hear thee sing thy songs of praise,
Amid the early, happy, girlish days,
That gave thee to my life a constant star,
Pointing my thoughts where kindred angels are.

We wandered down the hill-sides, and the flowers
Were redolent of thee, — their life was ours;
They drank the same clear dew, and the same air
That wooed their petals, made thy cheek as fair
As their sweet blossoms; the white lily stood,
In all her purity, near the dense wood,
And in the evening Zephyr bowed her head,
Inviting thee to her soft, lowly bed!

And the deep, bell-shaped flower of modest blue,
Told thee of friendships, tender, firm, and true;
And thy young, guileless heart did well respond
To truth and friendship, for thy soul was fond
As the maternal love to her first-born;
As tender as the smile upon that form
Of budding life; like the pure bliss of heaven,
To earth's unsullied, blessèd spirits given!

15

We knew not sorrow then, nor the pale blight
Brought by the years, in their swift, cruel flight;
We had not dreamed of the corroding care
That fills maturer life ; its burdens bear
Too heavily in the fast coming years,
When the worn heart is no more eased with
　　tears ;
Too heavily to let the joy remain,
That youth hath woven in its golden chain !

No more together shall we view the beams,
That flow in glory in the solar streams,
That flood the eastern hills ; nor in them view
The subtle threads that in our spirits grew
A woof of beauty, whose soft colors blend
In every phase of life, until the end :
But when the whispering spirits call me home,
Thy voice shall sweetly join to bid me come !

The valleys are as green, and the clear spring
To its cool fountain doth the lapwing bring ;
And the gay robin singeth round the door,
But thou, my sister, cometh back no more :
And every charm of earth, and every joy,
And every hour that doth my life employ,
Hath lost its fullness, for my star is fled :
Thou, thou, my sister, dwellest with the dead !

And yet not dead ! for thou dost oft return,
When evening's lamp doth camly, brightly burn ;

And when the bird of night doth sing of love,
Thy spirit whispers to me from above !
Amid the echoing rocks I faintly hear,
"Cheer up ! cheer up ! " like music from the
    sphere
Wherein thou dwellest ; and my soul is filled
With rapture, and my aching heart is stilled.

Calm evening ! unto thee alone is given
The brightest visions to the soul of heaven !
In thee the fond ones that have passed away,
Over the silent spirit hold their sway ;
And unto faith the heavenward breeze they bring,
That lendeth to its swift and upward wing
The mighty speed that eagles have not known ;
And I am with thee, sister, round the throne ! —

— Around the throne of love, where blossoms
    grow
In beauty, fading not, like these below ;
Where all the good, in every age and clime,
Drink purer pleasures, sinless and divine !
O, why do mortals cling to things below,
Which pass so quickly ? Why not wish to go
To better scenes, where parted spirits meet
With those they love, and join in chorus sweet ?

THE MANIAC.

I saw one, sad, and lone, and wild ;
A wasted one, Misfortune's child.
The passers-by looked lightly on,
Because they saw the light was gone —
The light of other days and years ;
Laughter and joy replaced with tears ;
With tears of sorrow often shed,
Yet easing not the weary head.

Behold him gazing on the sky, —
On distant visions passing by, —
Forever passing, never found. —
Faint music, of Æolian sound,
Approaches softly ; then away,
More distant ; as the moonbeams play
'Mid forest shadows, luring on
The traveller, till his hopes are gone.

I saw one murmuring ; but for what,
The wandering spirit telleth not ;
Perchance the bauble, the gay toy
That filled the childish heart with joy,
Was tempting on the sad one's feet ;
Then the maternal eye would meet
His own, and chiding, seem to say, —
" It is not thine, my boy ; away ! "

I heard him say, " I come ! I come !"
Ah ! he was dreaming then of home !
Of home ?   'Tis there the spirit clings,
As long as fitful reason flings
Her lucid halo round the heart,
Whose clinging tendrils cannot part
With sunny smiles, that ever there,
Chased tenderly the falling tear !

I heard him shrieking, — " No, no, no !"
From that sweet home he could not go ;
Ah ! hadst thou ever felt as now,
The wildness had not marked thy brow ;
The demon had not seized the throne,
That in the past was all thine own !
And never, till thy heartstrings break,
Shall the sad vision thee forsake !

Now thou art playing with the flowers,
Whose colors bring the youthful hours
As bright as they, as tranquil too,
As when the cooling, sparkling dew
Bathed them to freshness, when the sun
His fiery, ardent course had run :
No cooling dew thy cup shall fill,
Till the poor heart lies cold and still !

Behold him listening to the breeze
That rustles through the stately trees !

A faint smile lights the vacant eye,
As moaning, murmuring blasts sweep by !
Swift passing by, as passed the days
That witnessed all his childish plays ;
But never more shalt thou behold
The sunny, playful times of old !

I saw, O horror ! 'mid the roll
Of thunder, struggles of the soul !
As if the sudden, mighty crash,
The wildness of the lightning's flash,
Had torn asunder the strong strings
That bind the soul to meaner things :
And like the sun, the mighty mind
Looked forth revealed, but far behind ! —

— Behind the clouds, as is the sun
When he his garments putteth on ;
His sombre robes, his dim attire,
When hideth he his mighty fire.
But who will doubt, when storms shall cease,
When cometh he, in clear, sweet peace, —
O, who will doubt his glory then,
When storms, nor clouds, shall intervene ?

So shalt thou stand when storms are o'er
(When darkness shall divide no more
The mental view), revealed in peace,
With glory crowned, the soul's increase

Shall fill the blank of time, and thou
Shalt glorify thy God : e'en now,
That sudden light, that look from thee,
Presageth what thou then shalt be !

SNOW.

O, WHAT beautiful gossamer flakes
The down from the tree of heaven makes !
Pure as the fingers that shake the tree :
White as the garments the angels see !

Gently and softly it cometh down,
Giving the pines a beautiful crown !
Clothing their greenness with a white robe,
The fairest and purest e'er seen on the globe !

Spotless it cometh ! seeming to say, —
"Sinless the realms, as beams of the day,
Up where the loved ones, waiting to fly,
Look for the spirits cleaving the sky, —

"Look for the dear ones longing to go
Where the bright garments (white as the snow
On the green pine trees) wait for the soul
Wishing to go where the anthems roll !

"Beautiful home! sin dwelleth not there;
Sin with its sorrow, sadness, and care;
Up to the light! there knowing as known,
There, where the seeds immortal are sown.

"Up where they grow, nor blighted their bloom;
Shining forever! like a soft plume,
Fit for the angels, clustering seen
Growing together 'mid the dense green, —

"Covering the plains of beauty and bliss,
Up where the heavenly zephyrs shall kiss,
Tenderly, soothingly, every tear
Left on the eye while sorrowing here."

Beautiful snow, O linger till spring!
Linger until the beautiful green
Cometh in gladness, freshness, and love,
Pointing our hearts to the Eden above!

PRINCE.

BOUNDING, jumping, springing away !
Always blithesome every day ;
Summer and winter, hot or cold,
Trying to tell what never is told ; —
Trying to tell how happy is he,
Following where his master may be :
Asking no questions, feeling no doubt ;
Always a friend, in doors and out ! —

Always watching, awake and asleep ;
Dozing, but never slumbering deep ;
Sometimes dreaming all about me,
Sometimes barking up the wrong tree !
Sometimes thinking of the last bone,
Sometimes giving a sorrowful groan :
Doubtless sometimes shadows will flit,
Of some fair one, who gave him the mitt !

Happy is he when morning begins,
Holding his head (when tea-kettle sings)
All on one side ; just as though he,
Some straggling mouse wanted to see :
Watching the cupboard's open door,
Viewing the dishes wistfully o'er ;
Hoping a plate will soon be seen,
Waiting for him to lick up clean.

Swallowing down all that he finds, —
All but the bones : sometimes he grinds
Them with a zest, sucking them too
(Much the same way as the dear girls do
The dainty saccharine presents that flow
From each liberal, happy, and smiling young
 beau)
Quickly it's over, and waiting, he now
Looks up at his master, and makes his bow-
 wow !

Isn't he knowing for one who can't speak ?
When I scold him, he looketh so meek :
When I tell him supper is near,
Shakes he all over, looking so queer
Up in my face ! seeming to say,
" Come to the table, come, come away ! "
When I am sick, sorry is he,
Nestling, fawning, looking at me !
Haven't I said enough to convince
Every kind person they ought to love Prince ?

THOU SLEEPEST NOT.

HELPLESS, O Father! helpless, sore, and sad
Amid the storms, when all my hopes are clad
In disappointment: brooding o'er my lot,
The light breaks through, because Thou sleepest
    not:
And every fear that thought doth cheer, O God!

Rough is the road, O Father! but Thy hand
Doth lead me on, through all this barren land;
Weary, I find a resting-spot
Beneath the darkest cloud; — Thou sleepest not!
Thou, whilst I sleep, my soul dost keep, O God!

And when I wake, O Father! it is sweet,
Some fellow-traveller praising Thee, to meet;
So, when I rise with vigor from my cot,
I bless Thee then, because Thou sleepest not;
And I will praise Thee all my days, O God!

Sometimes I hear, O Father! distant sounds
Come floating softly, far beyond the bounds
Of my short vision! and my ear hath caught
The chorus of the song — "Thou sleepest not!"
That choral strain doth soothe my pain, O God!

Sometimes, O Father! noontide makes me faint
Beneath the heavy burden, and I pant

With thirst, for the high blazing sun is hot
Upon my head ; but O, Thou sleepest not !
Then Thou dost bring Thy sheltering wing, O God !

'Tis sweet to love Thee, Father ! sweet to know
Thou lovest me, while journeying here below.
Without thy love, my life were but a blot ;
Thy love is priceless, for Thou sleepest not !
Keep meek and mild, Thy favored child, O God !

I care not, Father, what the world may do
To me in life, if on my raptured view
Thy smile shall dwell ! It matters not, one jot,
If millions frown, because Thou sleepest not !
Twill not be long ere I am home, O God !

———◦◦◦———

ACROSTIC.

O, who imparted constant joy
Unto the heart that loves her boy,
Reclining where no cares annoy ?
Bo-peep every now and then,
At some familiar, loving ken !
Bliss for thee be ever in store ; —
Yea, forever, and evermore !